The Fictional World
of William Hoffman

The Fictional World of William Hoffman

Edited by William L. Frank

University of Missouri Press
Columbia and London

Library of Congress Cataloging-in-Publication Data

The fictional world of William Hoffman : edited by William L. Frank.
     p. cm.
    Includes bibliographical references and index.
    ISBN 0-8262-1275-1 (alk. paper)
    1. Hoffman, William, 1925—Criticism and interpretation. I. Frank,
William L., 1929–

PS3558.O34638 Z66 2000
813'.54—dc21

                                        99-058278

Designer: Vickie Kersey DuBois
Typesetter: Crane Composition, Inc.
Printer and binder: Thomson-Shore, Inc.
Typefaces: Cheltenham, Monoline Script MT

To Bill and to Beverly

He wrote; she believed.

Contents

Acknowledgments

The genesis of this book goes back a long way, and I owe a lot of people for getting me into the fictional world of Bill Hoffman. Since the last shall be first I begin by thanking each of the other contributors to this work. All busy professionally, all at the head of their class no matter what hat they wear at a particular time, each instantly agreed to participate in this project when I first approached them. We in turn all thank Bill Hoffman for his total cooperation and for allowing us to quote freely from his fiction. I am also indebted to one of my earlier graduate students, Mary Paige Hinton Davis, whose interest in Hoffman's work led to my first meeting with Bill and Sue Hoffman. Thanks to Bill and Steve Wall and Ken Woodley of the *Farmville Herald* for asking me to review Hoffman's novels and short-story collections for their readers, an association that goes back to 1970. Rob Vaughan of the Virginia Council for the Humanities and Public Policy supported the funding for a joint Longwood College–Hampden-Sydney College three-day symposium on Hoffman's fiction in 1988; five of the contributors to this work participated in that symposium.

I also thank George Core for permission to reprint Fred Chappell's essay, which originally appeared in *The Sewanee Review,* Mike Lund of the English Department at Longwood College, Louis Rubin for invaluable suggestions, Allen Wier of the University of Tennessee, and the Longwood College administration. In a very special way I want to express my warm gratitude to Billy Clark's administrative assistant, Tina Dean, for her expert secretarial assistance, and to my wife, Angie, for the patient hours she spent checking on the numerous quotations from Hoffman's fiction throughout the book. All of the fine folks from the University of Missouri Press, especially Beverly Jarrett, Jane Lago, and Julie Schroeder, deserve my heartfelt thanks for their support, suggestions, and patience. And Tim Trent and Rita Brandt of Longwood College's printing services have been most helpful.

Bill Frank
Longwood College

Note to the Reader

In this collection, each essayist's page citations to works by William Hoffman are to first editions, which, along with numerous helpful works pertaining to Hoffman's writing, are listed in the bibliography.

The Fictional World
of William Hoffman

Introduction

George Core

In the forty-five years of his career William Hoffman has written fifteen books of fiction that for range of effect—exactness of idiom, freshness of style, variety of characterization, thematic density, liveliness of humor, and tragic intensity—have seldom been equaled and only rarely exceeded in or out of the South in this country since World War II. At the time of this writing, Mr. Hoffman, who is now completing a sequel of *Tidewater Blood,* has published eleven novels and four collections of short stories.

Hoffman began by writing novels and did not turn seriously to the more demanding form of the story until he had four or five novels behind him. He hit his stride with short fiction after *The Death of Dreams,* his seventh novel, appeared in 1973. At least half of the stories reprinted in his first collection, *Virginia Reels* (1978), had first appeared after he had written *A Death of Dreams.* In slightly over a decade, beginning in 1988, he has published three more collections of short fiction: *By Land, by Sea; Follow Me Home;* and, in the spring of 1999, *Doors.* Now in his seventy-fifth year, Hoffman shows no evidence of slowing down. He has built up a considerable head of steam, and his vessel is heading at flank speed toward the open sea, not returning to port.

The novel, while the more difficult genre to create in terms of its sheer bulk, is in a technical sense less demanding and more forgiving than the story, as any real maker of fiction would say. For reasons that I will not attempt to explain, chiefly because I would be in the realm of pure speculation, Mr. Hoffman does not write either the long story or the short novel. His usual story runs from 6,500 to 8,000 words, and his average novel is about 150,000 words. Hoffman writes succinctly and economically even when he is poetic; he is no Faulkner or Wolfe who overwhelms the reader in a raging torrent of language. Even though he orchestrates his situations and themes and reveals his characters in various ways in his novels, he does not indulge in repetition and the other habits that make for what Henry James calls the "loose and baggy novel."

When it comes to the subjects, characters, themes, and genres that his fiction entails, Mr. Hoffman has seldom repeated himself in any way that could be considered disabling. He has written three novels that deal substantially with World War II, especially *The Trumpet Unblown* and *Yancey's War;* he has forged three novels that chiefly involve sin and the search for redemption—*A Place for My Head, A Walk to the River,* and *The Land That Drank the Rain;* in *The Dark Mountains* he has created a novel that adumbrates the clash between a dynasty and a labor union, and he has written another novel that superficially has much in common with it—*Tidewater Blood;* in *Furors Die* he has juxtaposed the rising and falling fortunes of two men, one well-bred and one not, in a manner that recalls *Yancey's War;* in one of his finest novels, *A Death of Dreams,* he has given an account of a burnt-out man in a gray flannel suit who is suffering from alcoholism and clinical depression; and finally, in *Godfires,* as in *Tidewater Blood* and other fictions such as *A Walk to the River,* he has designed and constructed a powerful mystery that keeps the reader turning the pages until the action rises to its culmination and the resolution is revealed.

Hoffman knows in his bones that little can drive a plot so well as a mystery. It is a mystery—Who killed Hamlet's father?—that propels the action of *Hamlet;* in *Crime and Punishment,* it is an entirely different kind of mystery—whether Raskolnikov's murder of the old pawnbroker and her sister will be exposed and proven. In the same way, murder and the murderer's identity stand at the heart of both *Godfires* and *Tidewater Blood.* Mystery, especially when it involves murder, need not be confined to popular novels—thrillers, police procedurals, detective stories—or even to the more complicated fictions that Graham Greene deems "entertainments."

The mystery, artfully presented, seizes the reader and won't release him or her until the mystery is solved and resolved; and so, as his understanding of fictive action has deepened, William Hoffman has become more and more inclined to plant a mystery at the heart of his plot. One senses that, for him, mystery in such novels as *Godfires* and *Tidewater Blood* provides the germ of the action and then becomes its motive force. He understands that the reader, carried along by the tide of events generated by the mystery and seeking its explanation and resolution, is fascinated—the intention of any good writer.

Edmund Wilson, in his role as literary curmudgeon and priest of high culture, may ask scornfully, Who cares who killed Roger Ackroyd?—but the readers of Agatha Christie and of many another author, including William Hoffman, care passionately. Wilson can complain about the subliterary level of detective fiction, but he realizes to some extent—partly through the agency of Somerset Maugham, Bernard DeVoto, and Joseph Wood Krutch—that "the detective story is the only department of fiction where pure story-telling survives." Wilson concludes his related pieces on this subject by deciding that reading detective stories is a vice "somewhere between smoking and crossword puzzles." But he never considers the possibility of how a mystery may propel the action of serious fiction by providing the narrative thrust and the element of causality that turns story into plot.[1]

Mystery is often allied with melodrama, a literary genre more complicated than many of us suppose. "The essence of melodrama," as Jacques Barzun writes of its regular appearance in Henry James's fiction, "appears as a deep conviction that certain deformed expressions of human feeling are evil and that this evil is positive and must be resisted." And so Barzun finds tragedy as a form of melodrama— the highest form; and he sees the "bulk of modern prose fiction, from Richardson to Balzac" as "aesthetic melodrama" and believes that James's fiction belongs in that category. To Barzun violence and exaggeration are central to melodrama, and he sees its primal force as encompassing an ever-present evil.[2]

Evil as a persistent, commonplace element in human experience— but by no means a negligible matter—coils and uncoils in the fiction of Hoffman and is the heart of his view of sinful and suffering humankind. The essence of this view of fallen man—original sin—derives from Calvinism. In a tribute to Madison Jones, a writer whose dark perspective on man rivals that of Thomas Hardy, Hoffman writes: "God's omnipotence and man's fall through original sin is bedrock. Mortals will be tempted, slip, and fall into iniquity. Some through grace will be granted salvation. Others will be cast into outer darkness."[3] This exact description of Calvin's stern view of the human condition may be found, mutatis mutandis, over and again in Hoffman's fiction as well as that of Jones and of a writer who has influenced both William Hoffman and Madison Jones—Robert Penn Warren.

1. Edmund Wilson's related essays on detective fiction—"Why Do People Read Detective Stories?" "Who Cares Who Killed Roger Ackroyd?" and "Mr. Holmes, They Were the Footprints of the Gigantic Hound!"—appear in his *Classics and Commercials: A Literary Chronicle of the Forties* (New York: Farrar, Straus and Giroux, 1950), 231–37, 257–74. See especially 261, 263.

2. Jacques Barzun, "James the Melodramatist," *Kenyon Review* 4 (autumn 1943): 510.

3. William Hoffman, "The Tempter Is Always with Us," *Chattahoochee Review* 17, no. 1 (fall 1996): 74.

The sense of evil that pervades and colors the action in Hoffman's fiction usually involves sex, often in perverted form. That applies to *Godfires, The Land That Drank the Rain,* and *Tidewater Blood* as surely as it does to Warren's *Brother to Dragons.* In *Tidewater Blood* the rape of the orphaned girl by Charles LeBlanc's father symbolizes the rape of the land by his coal company. LeBlanc violates the communion between nature and man, and his family pays a terrible price for his sins when it is almost eradicated by the blast at Bellerive. Only Charles and his brother Edward are spared; Charles by design, Edward by a fluke. It would be a relatively simple matter to trace comparable instances in Hoffman's fiction through which theme is exfoliated in action—for instance in *The Dark Mountains* and in *Furors Die* when a corporation plunders the land. When such a sin is carried out, someone must pay the old cost of the human redemption; for instance, in *Furors Die* Pinky Cody, in the course of his Icarian fall, loses his family, his money, and his life; and Wylie Duval is severely tested, being saved only by an inherited company. After the debacle Wylie thinks he may have seen the "haggard, robed" figure of Pinky's mother, "a raving woman whose hands were lifted in violent imprecation." Mrs. Cody, whose primitive religion continues to affect her son, despite his hard-won education and sophistication, calls down curses upon the modern world, whose values and behavior she abhors. Wylie does not ignore her, nor can we. She represents Fate as surely as does a Greek chorus.

The vise of old-time religion can still exert powerful force, as is obvious in such stories in *Virginia Reels* as "The Spirit in Me," an inverted saint's life. In Gormer the author presents his monstrous version of the saint, who, it will be recalled, is converted to God and received into the church after his early, often worldly and sinful, life; he then struggles against various temptations and has mystical experiences and performs miracles before culminating his life in holy death. Gormer, the self-appointed lay minister who handles snakes, follows this pattern in his grotesque fashion, being tempted by a woman while on a Greyhound bus and then flagellating himself with stones in a mountain stream: "I will be clean," he vows (5). Earlier he has undergone a mystical religious experience: "A blue light flashes before me and cracks like a thousand whips. . . . The ships crack through the mine, and a voice says, 'You are my instrument'" (3). Gormer thinks himself chosen by God, but instead he might be seen as singled out by Satan. As the story concludes, he carries out his own monstrous version of God's will in committing a double murder.

"The Spirit in Me" is an intense and powerful dramatization of the wages of sin and the complicated forces that religion can exert even today in a world that is largely post-Christian outside the mountains of West Virginia where this story unfolds. Hoffman presents light-hearted humorous versions of the same theme—the place of religion in the contemporary world—in such stories as "Amazing Grace" and "The Question of Rain." In "Sweet Armageddon," "Prodigal," and "Winter Wheat" he gives us dark variations on the theme of religion's enduring power—and not merely primitive religion. "Abide with Me," another such variation, entails a complicated mixture of humor and pathos in a Christian fable for our time.

William Hoffman's short stories, whether given to limning the intruder in the pocket society, as Fred Chappell describes it, or presenting the American Adam, as Gordon Van Ness tells us, often reveal, in succinct and incandescent forms, actions and themes that are developed more slowly and subtly in the novels. So it will be seen that "Your Hand, Your Hand" is a short version of *A Death of Dreams,* as is "Lover"; and "The Secret Garden," which explores a life of mental instability, develops in an intensely lyrical fashion the themes of promiscuity and madness, themes that play through *A Death of Dreams* in minor keys—leitmotifs. Ambition as a driving force is a theme that is embedded in the action of some stories and novels by Hoffman, especially *The Dark Mountains, Furors Die,* and "Expiation." Ambition is a powerful impetus that often becomes monomania, and other such manias play their roles in Hoffman's fictive world—the search for love, the dynastic impulse, violence and brutality (sometimes involving war but often not), the son's search for a missing or remote father, and so on. These themes are often intermingled, even interlocked, but Hoffman, like any other fiction writer worth his or her salt, has obviously not set out to explore each one in the systematic way that properly could be associated with sociology or psychology. Instead he has explored the theme or themes that have presented themselves when a given fable seized his attention. The story or novel often chooses the teller, who then must discover its full dramatic possibilities.

Stories begin in various ways, of course. Bill Hoffman has told me that for him, a short story sometimes gets under way when he hears the voice and idiom of the speaker—for instance, the narrator in "Moorings" who loses her husband. "I was Josie, Josie Catlett, and my fingers were cut so bad from shucking oysters that dishwater stung them till I danced at my sink" (97). So she introduces herself to us. And this is how she takes her leave: "As we stood by the grave, a southern breeze fanned whispering reeds, and silent, rain-washed gulls rode it like swells" (111).

Stories may also begin with images, such as the darkened room in the story of the same title, and the action may turn on an item central to its unfolding, such as the ancient furnace in "Doors," the posthole digger in "Tenant," or the black swan in "The Black Swan."[4] Such a physical object sometimes provides a controlling image for the action, and that is the case in "The Darkened Room" and "The Black Swan," as it is in "Roll Call" with the bugle given to the narrator by his uncle. We may be sure that when a writer finds an image to fix a point of stability in the drift of experience, he or she will use it to advantage, and following that image is a good way to understand how a given story works. On the other hand Mr. Hoffman's ability "to isolate common things," such as a posthole digger or pocketknife, yields what Warren calls, in praising Katherine Anne Porter for the same virtue, a "bright indicative poetry."[5]

Miss Porter herself has made it plain that fiction cannot depend upon mechanical and external symbolism—that instead it depends upon character and action. This brings us inevitably to Henry James. "Character," he observes, "is action, and action is plot, and any plot which hangs together, even if it pretend to interest us only in the fashion of a Chinese puzzle, plays upon our emotion, our suspense, by means of personal references." That, one of the great passages in the considerable bulk of James's criticism of fiction, appears in his essay on Trollope. The secret to fiction lies in character, what James, in writing of Turgenev, calls "character expressed and exposed." Hoffman has instinctively known this from the beginning, so that in his fiction the kinds of common items of ordinary life that I have specified are extensions of character and conduct, not items of great importance in themselves.

Let us linger for a moment on the action of "The Tenant." The narrator and protagonist cannot use a posthole digger properly, being a soft city boy, and so he hires Dexter Barlow; soon he is drawn into Dexter's violent and tawdry life. Dexter's story stands in startling contrast to the humdrum life of our narrator, who ironically is writing

4. *Sewanee Review,* winter 1999.
5. Robert Penn Warren, "Irony with a Center: Katherine Anne Porter (1941–52)," in *Selected Essays* (New York: Random House, 1958), 144.

a suspense novel with his wife while watching a suspense story unfold before his eyes. (The novel, we are not surprised to learn, does not find a publisher.) The action turns more nearly upon the lives of the narrator and his wife than it does upon Dexter and his former girlfriend, Windy Belle; but the stories of both couples are contrasted. "A character," as James says in his preface to *The Spoils of Poynton,* "is interesting as it comes out, and by the process and duration of that emergence." We watch that emergence as the complementary stories unfold: The narrator and his wife are trying to start a new life, while Dexter is ending his life and that of Windy Belle. Dexter has a bone-handled knife with a single long sharp blade, a knife with which he delicately peels an apple and later slits his wrists after he has strangled Windy Belle. There is little mystery in this murder and suicide; we have seen violence coming almost since Dexter entered the action. As is usual with a Hoffman story, the emergence of character is revealed in a series of short sharply focused scenes.

Hoffman's profound knowledge of common objects—clothing, hardware, tack, automobiles—demonstrates his wider knowledge of the places and professions that appear in his fiction. He knows how things work—and not merely simple items. He writes as well about the boardroom as he does about the Jenny Lind shack in a mining community; he knows the world of Chesapeake Bay and life on the water as well as life in the clubs and churches of Richmond; he can convey to the reader, in a few deft strokes, the gritty feel of quotidian existence in a country town or a mining village.

What William Hoffman is particularly adept at revealing fictively is the importance of money—or the lack of it—in society. Hoffman has the same subtle skill that Katherine Anne Porter praises in Henry James: He "understood and anatomized thoroughly and acutely the sinister role of money in society, the force of its corrosive powers on the individual." "The main concern," she continues, in "The Days Before," "of nearly all his chief characters is that life shall be, in one way or another, and by whatever means, a paying affair."[6] To trace the role of money as a paying affair through representative fiction by Hoffman would illuminate the workings of that fiction and reveal how he joins various fictive dimensions: the outer (or public) world with the inner (or private), the

6. Katherine Anne Porter, "The Days Before," in *The Collected Essays and Occasional Writings of Katherine Anne Porter* (New York: Delacorte Press, 1970), 244.

enveloping action with the action proper, fable and theme, and character and society. Such an intrinsic perspective as the role of money should define themes as they emerge from action. A simple version of money's role and the attitudes connected with it can be found in "Doors" in the clash of wills and values between the narrator, a comfortable—and snobbish—widow, and the proud repairman, Horace Puckett, who comes from a different social stratum than she. Much more complicated anatomies of its role can be found in the novels—*A Walk to the River, The Dark Mountains, Furors Die,* and *Tidewater Blood,* to name the most obvious. And in *The Land That Drank the Rain* the protagonist turns his back on capitalistic values and tries to find redemption in the simple life lived next to nature. Of course that turns out to be impossible. Ambition, a driving force in much of Hoffman's fiction, as we have seen, usually has money at its root.

We could examine still other aspects of Hoffman's fiction: the characteristic metaphors and other instances of poetry that color his prose and result in some of its most distinctive qualities; the exact idioms of the various segments of society in Virginia and West Virginia that Hoffman conveys with great accuracy and panache, a subject that Jeanne Nostrandt alludes to; the artfulness of his dialogue (in *Death of Dreams* on several occasions he presents a variation of stichomythia when Guy Dion tries to talk to others at the sanatorium, only to find they are on different wavelengths: this breakdown of communication as conversation continues can be hilarious, as in his last exchange with Cooley before Guy escapes); the relation of comedy and tragedy in his major work, such as *Yancey's War,* a matter that George Garrett explores; and the composition of his variegated world from West Virginia to southside Virginia (especially Tobaccoton) to Richmond to the Chesapeake locale, an element in Hoffman's fiction—place— touched upon by Dabney Stuart.

This collection of essays covers many important matters but necessarily cannot deal with all the essential aspects of this splendid writer's fiction. We leave other critical matters to other hands. The reader of this book will find that it is considerably more than an introduction to the distinguished accomplishment of William Hoffman. It contains strong essays on the best of the novels and many of the stories and shows what a talented writer Hoffman is. That until now he has been neglected on the critical front is both mysterious and unfortunate. This book of essays in criticism goes a long way toward getting Mr. Hoffman the attention that he has earned time and time again over a long and fruitful career.

Taking Measure

Violent Intruders in William Hoffman's Short Fiction

Fred Chappell

The term *pocket society* describes a definable aggregate of individual people that possesses recognizable dynamic qualities and important though often changeable relationships among its different members. It is smaller than our world or national societies or our body politic, and in the immediate sense it is more important to us because we engage so intimately and continually with it. Various pocket societies comprise our family, our professional colleagues, and the members of our church; the same is true of a bridge club or a sewing circle or an army barracks. But we rarely think about the natures of these small societies because they envelop us; we are caught up in their webs of multiple tensions and have no way to break clear and discover an objective point of view. We are too much a part of them; they are too much a part of us.

Fiction writers like to take a pocket society either as a foreground or a background subject. Its workings exhibit fascinating relationships, and its attitudes can demonstrate in striking fashion both human community and human solitude. For this reason, writers have devised a number of narrative strategies designed to bring to light the various strains and conflicts, passions and affections, hopes and fears that animate such groups. This kind of matter is more or less standard fare for the mainstream short-story writer.

Among these strategies of exposure one of the most useful is the introduction of an outsider into the pocket society, a figure whose presence makes overt what was covert, lays bare truths hitherto unknown or unacknowledged, causes the members of the society to take stock of one another and themselves and of the situation they inhabit. The title of Mark Twain's *The Mysterious Stranger* describes the nature of this kind of story—which is a very ancient one indeed. The Garden of Eden was a pocket society that remained untested, and therefore unknown, until the Serpent showed up.

William Hoffman is a sturdy traditional short-story writer; his four books of stories, *Virginia Reels; By Land, by Sea; Follow Me Home;* and *Doors,* are volumes I recommend happily to those readers of my acquaintance who inquire in sometimes plaintive tones, "Does no one

any longer write solid stories, the kind with plots and themes?"
Hoffman does, and in openhanded fashion. His relish for accessible
story lines, thematic clarity, informative detail, strong characterization, and satisfying structure is unmistakable. Almost any page shows
his enjoyment of these customary elements of fiction composition as
well as his quiet proficiency in their application. He rarely writes what
we could call an "experimental" story; he probably feels no need, being
so expert in the art of straightforward narrative.

It is his traditionalism, I believe, that draws him to tell this most familiar of stories, the intrusion of an outsider upon a pocket society.
His four volumes contain forty-two stories altogether and at least
nine of them are stories of interlopers. Perhaps five others could be
included in this count, but I fear to stretch my description by including such pieces as "Moon Lady," in which the mysterious stranger
who dances naked in the moonlight turns out to be the local post-
mistress, or "Moorings," in which an uptown couple from Norfolk
charms a poor harbor fisherman to his destruction with visions of
the easy life.

There is no need to include ambiguous examples because the ones
that are clear-cut comprise almost a fourth of Hoffman's collected
stories. And of these nine stories of intruders no fewer than six have
violence as a major element. This fact surprises me. William Hoffman
is not a melodramatic writer; even his military novels do not depend
upon bloodshed for their emotional force. But his short stories "The
Spirit in Me," "The Darkened Room," "A Walk by the River," "Tides,"
"Night Sport," and "Business Trip" all employ violence or the close
threat of violence. It is not garish shoot-'em-up comic-book mayhem
and Hoffman is not spatteringly graphic, yet violence is indispensably
present upon his pages and provides energy and suspense in edgy
plenteousness.

He does not always require violence to give his "interloper" stories
force. In "Sweet Armageddon," the one who intrudes upon the lives of
the outcast minister, Amos, and his wife, Martha, is an old college
buddy. His nickname is "Whale," and his deed is benevolent in intention rather than abusive; he invites his friend to breakfast at his plush
private club. Though for the straightly religious Amos the meal is
more ordeal than treat, he endures it with as much dignity and affa-
bility as he can muster. When he returns home from his too-opulent
meal, he finds his elderly wife sitting lonely at the kitchen table, deal-

ing solitaire with a deck of handsome cards, "perhaps from a sorority or bridge club, a deck from another life." Amos observes once more that her actions and her setting are unfit for her background, that her unwavering love for him has brought her to a pinched and gloomy existence. "Her fingers were so fragile, made for the holding of roses and fine porcelain" (77).

This sentence shows Hoffman's Chekhovian leanings; the intruder stories that lack violence often imply a debt to the Russian master. "A Southern Sojourn" dramatizes the power that loneliness and boredom have upon even a highly educated and well-intentioned person and of the sour disruption that can result. In this story an engineer is sent from Minnesota to a small town in Virginia to oversee the installation of a boiler in a new knitting mill. The evenings are long and he tries hard to keep occupied, but so much free time is too onerous a burden. Finally he initiates an affair with a young black woman, a college dropout who is unwilling to let herself be used in this fashion. But she is dreadfully poor and she becomes not the man's whore but his paid mistress; the distinction is perhaps a fine one but important to both of them.

Neither is happy with the arrangement, and the woman gives Orson no peace. Once, when he hands her twenty dollars, Eunice says, "You must think I'm choice meat. You must think I'm tenderloin" (105). There can be no solution to the problem; each of them is already married and, besides, the attraction they feel towards each other is not the kind that good marriages are based upon. Their needs are so different their hearts could never be consonant. From the beginning they have foreseen the end; Orson will be called away, Eunice will be abandoned. Orson tries hard to see the episode as something different from what it has been. The last time they meet he asks Eunice if she ever came to him for his own sake or always only for the money. She counters by asking the same question: "Did you want me because of me? Or do you think you're kind and noble?" (110).

Like "Sweet Armageddon," "A Southern Sojourn" affords no new revelation; the characters only experience an intensification of the knowledge and feelings they have already been living with. When the parting comes for Orson and Eunice there is no tearful farewell, not even a bittersweet goodbye, but only a laconic acknowledgment of the meaninglessness of their relationship. As he drives away forever, he spots her at one of her daily tasks, burning trash in a wire incinerator. "He stopped the car to wave to her. She didn't see him, or pretended not to. . . . She emptied the can, stepped away from the flames, and went inside" (111).

"A Southern Sojourn" has no resolution beyond this moment of inarticulate frustration; it ends with a stalemate that suggests some of the most uncomfortable aspects of our national race problem. Orson, the Yankee intruder, has only intensified a bad situation that was already in place.

In other stories, however, the intruder can bring about some measure of resolution. In "Tides," a father and son, Wilford and Dave, are taking their sailboat *Wayfarer* from Albemarle Sound to the Chesapeake Bay. Dave has just graduated from Duke University, has landed a management trainee position with a bank, and is about to get engaged to a girl. All these developments—and especially the last—relieve some of Wilford's concerns about his son: "As a child the boy had been frail, allergic to foods, plants, insects. During college he'd become interested in theater and talked of becoming an actor-playwright. Friends Dave brought home had been definitely faggy. Wilford struggled to prevent certain pictures from forming in his mind, though prepared to stand by his son come what might. The filling satisfaction was to have him as he was now" (22).

This celebratory excursion is interrupted by an intruder, a nasty customer who abducts the pair at gunpoint and orders them to sail him to Baltimore. He means business and, though he knows nothing about boats or sailing, is alert and cunning. He sees through every stratagem that crosses Wilford's mind and asserts his authority by pistol-whipping the father. When Dave attempts to attack him with a flare gun, his plan goes awry and the criminal orders the young man off the boat and into the bay to drown. Wilford pleads, offering to exchange his own life for his son's, but Dave forestalls his father. "To Wilford's horror, Dave wailed and did a shameful thing. As he begged, he reached to the man's foot and kissed it. He kept kissing the foot" (39).

In this moment all the anxieties about his son's virility come to the fore. Wilford loves Dave, although he is not someone who can speak his emotions openly. "He'd always assumed the intensity of his feelings for the boy would beam out, radiate, make themselves known" (21). In fact, part of Wilford's purpose in this celebratory voyage has been to try to communicate his feelings. "Perhaps before they headed south again, he could summon words to make the appreciation of his son official" (21). His doubts about Dave's masculinity have prevented his opening his heart and now in this moment of violent crisis these same doubts almost prove the undoing of them both. He watches horrified as his son kisses the gunman's foot, but he has misunderstood the situation: "Cursing, the man stepped back off balance. On his belly Dave thrust after him and shouted, 'Grab him, Dad!'" (39).

They overpower their abductor; in the struggle, Dave loses a front tooth. As he starts to pitch it overboard his father takes it from him, intending to keep it always, the way parents preserve their children's baby teeth. Wilford goes to correct the boat's course ("a father's habit"), but then halts himself and gives control to Dave: "He pulled back and dropped the hand to the throttle, which he pushed full forward. *Wayfarer* had plenty of water under her and a good man at the helm" (40).

Unlike "A Southern Sojourn" and "Sweet Armageddon," "Tides" is a fully resolved story. Its violent climax makes resolution possible. Wilford's unspoken and largely unconscious uncertainties about Dave come to the surface and are dissipated in one swift triumphant moment, and without this melodramatic incident his doubts might have remained to nag at him for years.

I must say, however, that I do not find the agent of this violence convincing. He seems more a figure from film or television than a real person: "The man wore a Panama hat, a tightly fitted khaki suit, and a maroon tie over a purple shirt. His full black mustache seemed much too large for his face. His skin was sweat shiny, particularly scar tissue curved across a cheek" (22). His dialogue also sounds stagy: "'You ever been to Baltimore?' he asked. 'You'll love that whore of a city'" (26).

Yet elsewhere Hoffman can draw villainous types with broad colorful strokes, characters that loom in the memory as full of menace as when first met on the page. Foremost among them must be Gormer, the snake-handling fundamentalist lay preacher of "The Spirit in Me." In this story, told from Gormer's point of view, the intruder is the unnamed heiress of a coal magnate:

> She comes from Virginia west to ancestral acres, a jagged country of rock outcroppings and mountains gutted and scarred. She rests in deep shade at the mansion her great-grandfather built, three stories of dungeonlike stone topped by a copper roof which glints in noon sun. She comes with sin. (1)

In this story it is the point of view that identifies the intruder. The woman of the mansion visits here only in the summers. The land belongs to the company she owns, but Gormer's church is established on it, "a board-and-batten building hammered together by my father, the roughness of new lumber first against his hands and then against my own" (1). Gormer helped his father erect the church and has proprietary feelings about the ground it stands upon. He tells the deputy sheriff who has been sent to evict him, "It is my church." The deputy replies: "You may think it's yours, but the law says the land and building still belong to the company." Gormer's answer is the one he has ready for all such occasions of conflict: "I am an instrument, and the Holy Spirit works through me" (11).

The author gives us to know that there is something besides the Holy Spirit working through, and within, Gormer. His father, before dying in a mine accident, had instructed his son in his own terrifying religious faith, and his mother has prayed—"Take my boy and use him!" (4)—that her son will follow the ways of his father. His father's doctrine and the manner of his death and the desperate fervor of his mother combine to shape Gormer's character and to provide the revelation of his vocation:

> I am afraid of dreams and the stains on myself. No water washes me clean. That summer I go into the mountain, into the wet blackness of the mine which has the sulphuric smell of the pit. The first day as I work setting locust props to hold the roof, a blue light flashes before me and cracks like a thousand whips. All the hair is singed from my body. I am thrown on the haulway floor among gobbets of coal. The whips crack through the mine, and a voice says, "You are my instrument!" (3)

Gormer is, of course, the most unreliable of narrators. The experience he recounts is real to him, including the singeing of his hair, and so he is unable to know how powerfully his upbringing informs all his perceptions. Other factors besides overbearing parents and cramped religious thoughts are also in force. He has absorbed, all unknowingly, his father's envy of the mine owners: "'They was common once!' my father rages when they arrest him because of snakes. 'The old man didn't have a pisspot when he first come to these mountains. My grandfather fed him. He'd have starved the winter withouten my grandfather's hog and hominy!'" (3).

Gormer is so sexually repressed that in one quick episode he badly injures a tipsy woman who makes a trial of his virtue, and he is so abysmally lonely that he takes his highly dangerous church companions to be his "children":

> Now I have children of my own, not from a wife, but from the Spirit. I feed and treat them tenderly. They lie among clean curls of wood shavings which rustle slightly. During spring and summer I harvest young rabbits hanging in my snares.
>
> My children know me, the heat of my hand, and they raise their heads when I lower meals to them. They know my fingers when I lift them from their box. I hold them as gently as wafers. (5)

Gormer never speaks explicitly of the contrast between his own miserable way of life and that of the coal heiress, but Hoffman manages to make clear the savage envy that possesses him. The heiress is a widow whose husband died in war, and the other citizens of the settlement praise her civic-minded charity in full chorus. When one of them recalls that she helped the town to get water, Gormer responds, "It is not the water of life" (6).

The episode that climaxes the story is one of sexual jealousy. A fair number of Hoffman's stories are concerned with voyeurism; sometimes the voyeurs are only passive watchers, sometimes they harbor inimical plans. "The Darkened Room," "Lover," "Moon Lady," "Altarpiece," and "Boy Up a Tree" all contain voyeurist scenes and a number of other stories refer to the act. In "The Spirit in Me" the situation is strongly and deliberately reminiscent of the Bible story of a paradise with its natural free sexuality and an embittered intruding serpent. In the final scene the widow has invited a male guest to dinner and for a swim in the lake afterward. Gormer watches for a long while, then goes to his house, returns with a package, and begins to watch once more:

> I return with the box. Biting my breath, I kneel among laurel. She and her man swim in from the float. They rise from the dark water. She starts away, but he reaches after her and draws her. In moon I see him put his mouth on her. She holds to him as he unties the top of her bathing suit. He kisses her, and I whimper. Her hands are splayed over his temples. He lifts and carries her into the bathhouse. A click causes light to die. (14)

Because the story is told from Gormer's point of view and because his range of vision is so excruciatingly narrow, "The Spirit in Me" offers little room for a reader to gain perspective upon the situation as a whole. The villagers with their litany of praise for the woman give some broad notion of what she is actually like, yet Gormer's outlook is so dark and tainted and intense in expression that it is hard to stand back from it. But one remark of Gormer's tells more about him than any amount of authorial exposition ever could: "He kisses her, and I whimper."

That is a master sentence. It readies us for the sudden ending in which Gormer secures all the exits of the bathhouse while the amorous couple is inside. He also cuts off the electric power and then accomplishes his plan: "Kneeling on the wooden steps, I lovingly feed my children through the doorway. They flow off my palms into darkness" (14).

Figures like Gormer are hardly uncommon in southern literature and have been limned with wonderful skill by Davis Grubb, Harry Crews, Madison Jones, and other writers. But I think no one has done the job so deadly and with such deft economy as William Hoffman. "The Spirit in Me" is a nightmare as deep and dark as they come, but it finishes in fourteen pages.

In fact, few of Hoffman's stories are much longer than twenty pages, and sometimes it appears a bit of a struggle for him to fit everything in. "A Walk by the River" in *Virginia Reels* feels cramped; too many incidents are crowded into a small space—an encounter with a young tough and his hippie girl friend, a theft by the young man, a sexual episode between the girl and the protagonist, the return of the tough and a subsequent robbery, a shift in the allegiance of the girl.

But for the most part the lengths of these stories are satisfying. They are lean but strong, moving with quick grace from point to point, and when they conclude, the figure they have shaped is a memorable and pleasing one. Much of their impact derives from brevity; I have mentioned Chekhov as a writer who surely has influenced Hoffman, and I think he must also have read his Kipling.

"Business Trip," in *Follow Me Home*, is as laconic a story as "A Walk by the River" and, though it presents fewer incidents, contains as many surprises. These are skillfully handled and do not tumble over one another; they proceed in a smooth taut sequence, and the final revelation they produce is not only—as it first seems—of one character's hidden nature but of a much larger situation.

Here the pocket society contains only two individuals, the un-named narrator and his friend Harrison, a couple of grouse hunters inordinately proud of their sport and extremely protective of their partnership. They have built a purposefully Spartan cabin in the mountains and when they invite other hunters as their guests—something they very rarely do—they subject them to a ruthless scrutiny: "We were damn particular whom we invited each season. First, a guest had to be serious in his pursuit of grouse. Second, he had to see hardship as homage to the king of birds. Third, the guest needed to find joy in adversity. Last, in the high country truth pre-vailed" (157–58). This latter demand is pompous and hubristic, and it is fulfilled in a way the narrator could never have predicted or de-sired.

Circumstances alter cases, the old saw tells us, and the two men are forced to bend their rules to accommodate the presence of Clarence Toller. Clarence is a soft effeminate man and evidently no Nimrod, but he is the employer of Trixie, the narrator's wife, and she prevails upon her husband to allow Clarence to accompany the two men as their unwanted third partner. The deciding factor is money. Trixie's job is necessary for the couple to keep up the standard of liv-ing to which they are accustomed; she has been forced to work for their second income because of an unwise political choice on the part of her husband, and now she must keep in the good graces of her boss.

The trial is a sore one. Clarence is everything a macho man is not. Harrison suspects him of being "a fag": "'Manicured nails, silver cuff links, cologne, and way he sits with his knees together. Bet he has pa-jamas'" (163). Clarence has indeed brought pajamas, "white with red horizontal stripes, and a bathrobe and slippers" (164). He is also frightened of the woods in the nighttime, anxious about the lack of indoor plumbing, careless with firearms, clumsy-footed, squeamish about killing game, and unable to eat the birds the others shoot. They are not surprised when on the second day Clarence chooses not to go into the woods but to stay in the cabin reading a book related to his antiques business, *Early American Silversmiths.*

But on the third day he decides to try his sporting skills once more, and when the other two split up to pursue separate trails he accom-panies the narrator. Almost as soon as they are alone Clarence brings up the subject of Trixie. She has been thinking, he says, of leaving her husband. The narrator counters that this is no one's business but their own and then, while they are bickering, a grouse breaks cover. Clarence brings it down with an expert shot. He turns out to be an excellent marksman, and explains why: "'Daddy had all us redneck boys out hunting as soon as we could carry guns. When you killed your first buck deer, they made you cut its throat, gut it, and drink a cup of hot blood. I puked and shamed Daddy.'" He parries the narrator's astonishment with an offhand but sinister comparison. "'Shooting's like screwing,' he said and winked. 'You don't forget'" (173).

Expert though he is, Clarence does not enjoy hunting game. He calls the sport "ridiculous macho madness," a "Daniel Boone charade" (173). He reveals that his true purpose in joining the hunters was to find an opportunity to broach the subject of Trixie. "She needs tender loving care, which you're not providing," he says. "So I've been hoping to help" (174). When the narrator balks at this suggestion Clarence attempts a more urgent sort of persuasion, raising his Browning in the other's direction. The narrator is taken aback but not finally convinced: "You're being stupid, I told myself. Afraid of a damn queer" (174). But now the possibilities become precipitately less moot. "'You read about hunting accidents,'" Clarence says. "'Harrison would be an expert witness. He'd honestly testify what a booby I am in the woods. What jury would convict a sweetie like me!'" (175).

The climax of "Business Trip" is a gunshot. No one is injured, but the narrator is so frightened by it that he wets his pants and flings his Parker shotgun away. Clarence retrieves it: "'Look what I found!' he called. 'Look what I discovered!'" He has discovered not only the expensive firearm but the narrator's true character. Finding that he has become a prey animal, the narrator disgraces himself. His bravado attitude does not sustain him and it is clear that he is going to lose everything to a hunter whose like he has never imagined before. The episode has fulfilled in brutally ironic fashion the most stringent demand of this pocket society: "Last, in the high country truth prevailed."

In "Business Trip" the society intruded upon by Clarence consists of only two men, but Hoffman has written at least a couple of stories, "The Darkened Room" and "Night Sport," in which the pocket society is made up of a single individual. Both of them are tense and disturbing stories and both contain thieves as characters. And in both cases it is the thief who comes to understand—too late—the meaning of the situation he has intruded upon.

"Night Sport," from *Virginia Reels,* tells the story of a veteran named Chip who has lost his legs in the war in Vietnam. The chronicle of his embittered withdrawal from his family, his friends, and the other comforts of social life is powerful, and all the more so because Chip's motives are not revealed until the end of the story. He has moved out of his well-off parents' rather grand house in order to live in squalor in a small cottage that he purposely allows to acquire a rundown, almost abandoned, appearance. Chip arms himself with an L. C. Smith double-barreled shotgun and with a generous supply of whiskey, and waits.

At last an intruder arrives; it is a student from St. John's, "a private Episcopal academy housed in Georgian buildings and surrounded by grassy playing fields." The school is expensive and traditional: "Life was patterned after English schools, with emphasis on classics and sports. Students wore blazers and ties to class. . . . Young southern gentility being formed" (130). The student, whose name is Tommy, has broken into Chip's house in order to steal a television set; the act is part of his initiation into John's Jesters, one of the clubs of the academy. "'Initiation requires you have to do something daring,'" Tommy explains (130).

His explanation, and the long, deceptively friendly chat that follows it, take place at gunpoint. Chip keeps his shotgun trained upon the young man as they discuss campus clubs, tea dances, track and field sports, and Tommy's future plans. He intends, he says, to go to Washington and Lee; Chip had attended the University of Virginia after his years at St. John's. The conversation is polite, almost casual, according to Tommy's perception. He cannot know what Chip is thinking:

> The little prick felt not only sorry for but also superior to him. The new breed, chosen, anointed, the slickies he saw tooling around the shopping center with blue-lidded piglets in rock-pounding Corvettes and TransAms. Righteous little farts. He stiffened as if about to be scorched again by the great exploding truth. Goddamn it, they ought to have to learn. They needed to know. (134)

Chip, like the religious zealot Gormer in "The Spirit in Me," believes that he is possessed of a truth, one great truth that gives him justification to make it known to the world in any way he pleases and at whatever cost. Chip's fervor is not religious, but it is a faith nonetheless and, like Gormer's, twisted into as terrifying a shape by his own personal history—by the things he has witnessed and experienced, by the loss of his legs.

The rundown cottage Chip inhabits has been a trap; he had expected that he would snare a thief with it, though he had not expected his prey to be so thoroughly to his desires. With his reminiscent palaver about prep school and college Chip has only been toying with Tommy in cat-and-mouse fashion. He starts to send him away with a knife that would prove the boy had actually effected entry into his house, then casually calls him back at the last moment:

> As Tommy turned back politely, Chip thumbed the L. C. Smith's safety forward. He pulled each trigger, firing the right barrel for Tommy's left calf, the left barrel for the right—the shells No. 8 dove load. Tommy's legs were slammed back beneath him. The front length of his body pounded the floor. . . . Dazed and astonished, he lifted his head, and the terrible knowledge, the deepest knowledge of all, flowed into those honey brown eyes. He struggled to right himself, howled, and now sobbing on his side, hinged forward as if exercising to touch his toes. (135)

After shooting Tommy, Chip tosses his victim a towel, then telephones the sheriff's office to send an ambulance, saying that his house has been broken into by a knife-wielding burglar. After telephoning, he raises the window blinds, turns on the house lights and gathers in the mail and newspapers he has allowed to accumulate on his front porch. He obliterates any impression that his house could have been intended as a baited trap. Like Clarence in "Business Trip," Chip gets away with his deception scot-free.

Many stories that deal with one-person societies are *contes cruels.* Edgar Allan Poe is the master of this subgenre, and "Night Sport" has more than an incidental resemblance to "The Cask of Amontillado," while "The Spirit in Me" is similar to "The Tell-Tale Heart." "Your Hand, Your Hand," Hoffman's story of alcoholic nightmare, is a bit reminiscent of "The Pit and the Pendulum." These are all stories in which a single individual is subjected to an ordeal he can neither comprehend nor escape. Their unfolding is hypnotic, their power horrific; they reveal the utter helplessness of the isolated person.

"The Darkened Room," one of Hoffman's strongest tales, is a neat variation upon the familiar theme. It begins, however, in a most familiar way: a young thief named Richard is spying on the house of a rich but dissolute married couple. Like the murderous preacher Gormer, his malevolent motives stem from his family history. His mother is a nurse, bitter and resentful of the husband who deserted her. "He cheated me out of my life," she tells her son. "He lied, robbed, and gave me a filthy disease from his whoring. . . . I wish I'd killed him. I wish I could put a knife in him right now. And you're like him!" (34).

After meticulous preparation, and making sure that the couple has left to attend a party, Richard breaks into the house he has scouted. Hoffman builds considerable suspense as he describes the thief's progress from room to room, his careful caution and his skilful stealthiness. But, like Tommy in "Night Sport," Richard has entered a situation he does not understand. When he enters the last room, the one he has observed to remain dark always, the light snaps on, and he finds himself in the presence of "a fat old woman who sat in a high-backed cane wheelchair" (38). She is a figure so grotesque that Richard tastes vomit and almost fouls himself:

> She bulged through the chair, and it dented her flesh. She wore a black, powder-dusted dress which had buttons missing, cotton stockings, and flowered bedroom slippers that were split along the seams. Her legs were as thick at the ankles as at the knees. Creases of her face were so deep they held shadows. On her neck was a growth which lapped over her white collar to her shoulder. Kinks of white hair grew from a flaking pinkish scalp. Her green eyes had chips of darkness in them. Her lashes and brows were gone. (38)

This strange woman is the mother of the house owner. She is the house's shameful secret, hidden away from all eyes but the family's. Richard's presence does not alarm her; she has seen too much hardship and violence in her life to be frightened of the young man, even when he threatens her. She tells Richard that he is unable to harm her. "'You won't because you're afraid to touch me'" (40).

It is the daughter-in-law who keeps her prisoner, the old woman says. "'She's afraid people will find out we're coal camp. When her friends come, she pulls the blinds and locks me in the room. She won't let me eat at the table evenings. Why she'd turn to rain water and sink right into the ground if any of her new friends saw me'" (44).

She sides with Richard, but her motive is not revenge upon her son and daughter-in-law. Her allegiance to the thief seems instinctive, a bonding, a recognition of their kinship as shameful miserable outcasts. The difference is that she is old and has seen through the sham of false expectation while Richard still hopes to elude his destiny. When the couple returns home from the party, quarreling loudly and drunkenly, she helps Richard escape capture in the house. Pride is the reason she gives for her action:

> "I know I'm a burden. . . . What a lot of people want is for me to drop into the grave, but it's my pride I won't. Us Ackers has always been gifted with long life. I'll sit here in the dark and not show myself, but I won't go to the grave till a team of angels' mules drags me. It's my pride." (44)

Under the hoard of parvenu wealth sits this grotesque and abandoned old woman, the dirty secret at the heart of a false economy, hidden away out of shame and because of her origins that have long been denied but cannot be forgotten. She is there always to remind her son and daughter-in-law of what and who they really are; she is the truth they cannot forget but cannot admit to, and it is the hypocrisy in regard to her existence that is ruining the lives of the married couple. All their money cannot rescue them.

This is the truth the old woman knows and has tried to demonstrate to the housebreaker. But Richard is too young; his situation is so desperate that he must harbor some hope, however forlorn and blind. He evades arrest and makes his way home by a circuitous route and goes to bed. He is safe from the police and from that unhappy house with its terrible secret. But he is not safe from the torture of hope, and sleep does not come easy: "He finally slept but woke during the night. It was still snowing. The horn of a coal tug sounded along the muffled river valley. His right hand was stretched up into darkness toward the hill as if there were something for him to touch" (45).

Here, as in other stories by Hoffman, the traditional trope of microcosm-macrocosm is put to good use. The situation that Richard discovers when he breaks into the pocket society of a wealthy house mirrors in small a larger situation in our national society. The microcosm-macrocosm metaphor is well suited to the tradition-oriented talents of Hoffman and he employs it with admirable results in stories like "Indian Gift," "Smoke," "A Southern Sojourn," "Sea Treader," and a number of others.

But it is perhaps most effective in those stories where an act of violence exposes, as suddenly and nakedly as switching on a klieg light, the underlying scaffolding of the framework in which it takes place. Inexpressive in itself, the violence brings to sharp focus truths that go generally unremarked in the course of daily events. Whether sordid, as in "The Darkened Room," or pitiable, as in "Night Sport," or sanguine, as in "Tides," these truths are always present, but they require the right kind of incident to lend them the force of revelation. It is difficult to give violence in fiction any stronger value than the merely sensational, but William Hoffman is an author equal to the task. He is more than equal to this one requirement; he is the master of it—and of many others.

The American Adam in the Southern Wasteland

William Hoffman's *Follow Me Home* and the Ethics of Redemption

Gordon Van Ness

William Hoffman's third collection of short stories, *Follow Me Home,* constitutes a continuation of his earlier volumes, *Virginia Reels* and *By Land, by Sea.* Hoffman's protagonists have almost always been outsiders, men and women who reject the traditional values sanctioned by society; they keep their own counsel and act on their own beliefs. This intense individualism, at times solipsistic, often warps their moral consciousness, and they become grotesques, having so accepted their personal values or so distorted commonly held ethical standards that, in their envy or resentment, they resemble the biblical figure of Cain, not so much losing their innocence as never seeming to have possessed it. Their self-serving and self-justified actions condemn them, as it were, to a moral wasteland they themselves have created, a world distinctly southern in geography, in which personal gratification in what they do becomes synonymous with personal redemption.

This attitude is particularly true in *Virginia Reels,* a darkly pessimistic collection of stories where Hoffman's strict Presbyterian upbringing reveals itself through its Calvinist depiction of good and evil. Mr. Gormer, for example, the narrator in "The Spirit in Me," possesses fundamentalist religious beliefs, including the handling of poisonous snakes, that set him apart from the rest in his rural community in the Virginia mountains. His inability to resolve his inner conflicts and his literal adherence to biblical injunction result in his loosing his "children" (5) on an amorous young couple he has locked in a boathouse. His spiritual corruption is nowhere better stated than in Hoffman's final sentence, where Gormer effectively damns himself through his smug self-righteousness and his lack of human compassion: "As I walk toward the forest I hear her gasp. I do not turn even at the first scream" (14). Similarly, in "A Darkness on the Mountain," Roy's courtship of Anna Mae and his dislike of Buster, a "heller" (86), result in his tying his rival deep within a mine shaft. Like Gormer, he walks away, and though he believes Buster lies "in a darkness that never lifted" (94), he is blind to the fact that he himself walks in an ethical darkness deeper than that of any mountain.

Hoffman's presentation of human nature becomes less severe in his next collection, *By Land, by Sea,* though his characters continue to act according to and on behalf of their own self-interests. Published a decade after *Virginia Reels,* these stories still depict outsiders moti-vated either by a corrupt (and corrupting) spiritual certainty or by their physical needs. In "Lover," for example, Dave lives a regimented and sterile life that masks his desperate efforts to deny age. A success-ful business manufacturer whose wife, Helen, has died some seven years earlier, Dave first shadows and then rapes a young woman, need-ing her youthfulness to affirm his own vitality. "I must live it one last time," he declares, "the youth and Helen, the hope, the promise of glory, the soaring" (81). As he waits for the police to arrive in the isola-tion of his materially comfortable but emotionally perverted home, he recognizes his own differences from others: "They will come for me, yet no matter how I explain, they'll never believe what I have done is out of love" (82). Such a recognition sets him apart from Gormer and Roy, who have no real sense of themselves and who never attempt any psychological or sociological analysis. Yet in his surrender to personal need, an ethic of selfishness, Dave belongs with the grotesques who people *Virginia Reels.*

However, *By Land, by Sea* also depicts another sort of figure, also an outsider but not a spiritual grotesque. While he remains solitary, often a refugee from society who now lives by choice in self-imposed exile from it, his independence is a source of strength. Earlier charac-ters also possessed this freedom, but it acted upon them, as it were, either to heighten their need for retribution or justice or to deepen their sense of alienation, thereby causing them to further their per-sonal values by using others. Hoffman's new protagonist still pos-sesses the self-reliance that enables him to endure; however, his selflessness, or what might simply be labeled Christian charity, as-sures that he will persevere. In *By Land, by Sea,* for example, Dave's selfishness in "Lover" is countered by Peck's effort in "Altarpiece" to extend love to one more isolated than he; rather than taking, he of-fers. Peck's wife, like Dave's, is dead. However, instead of remaining among the memories as Dave does (even using his wife's clothing as an excuse to bring the woman he rapes into the stately house), Peck leaves, selling his Cumberland farm, giving much of his material possessions to his children, and contracting with an auctioneer to dispose of the remainder (his wife's clothes go to Goodwill). Haunted by the words in his wedding vows, "Whom God has joined together, let no man rend asunder," he flees to his small and economical Chesapeake cottage, though later, as the memories flood back and leave him "run over and bleeding" (130), he drives three hours one night to lie across his wife's grave. His values and attitudes require him to reach out to Jenny, a bereft woman whose own sorrows exceed his: "So much trouble, so much misery for Jenny," he thinks, "those husbands, a wayward daughter, the frantic attempts to hold things together by selling cosmetics. He pictured her brave smile beneath those desperate eyes" (136). When his shyness and formality cause him to jerk free as she tries to kiss him, he is genuinely shocked to see the total despair into which she falls after she leaves him: "He'd never witnessed such sorrow, not even in himself—a pain that wrenched and shrank her body. She flinched as if being flogged. Her mouth's wail was soundless through the beaded window. Her suffering, he believed, came not from him alone. Rather, his rejection of her on the porch had been but the last step down a pitiless slope to a final, all-conquering despair" (142). This revelation transforms Peck, and as he now hears the words of a new vow—"Whom grief has joined . . . Whom grief has joined" (143)—he reaches out to her, literally and figuratively, as the story concludes, finally understanding that love redeems.

Such compassionate figures dominate *Follow Me Home*—women and men who know themselves and who possess in their hearts a treasure of values that separates them from society on the one hand but which provides them a spiritual richness on the other hand. It is not that these figures remain ignorant of the fallen world around them, failing to see the invasive and debilitating morality against which they have set themselves. Rather, it is as if the values by which they live and to which they have committed their lives serve to free them from the attitudes and actions that derive from modern life, where money and materialism have replaced manners and corrupted the will to excellence. In their innocence the characters consequently resemble Adam, not Cain, in the world as it were but not of it, who find or who have already found an inner paradise. In their ethic of self-reliance and adherence to old-fashioned values that ironically have become new in the southern wasteland where they live, Hoffman's protagonists find redemption, a spiritual wholeness. Like Adam, each character in

Follow Me Home is alone, an individual who stands—and acts—in this fallen world, depicting the traits or characteristics identified by R. W. B. Lewis in *The American Adam:* "an individual emancipated from history, happily bereft of ancestry, untouched and undefiled by the usual inheritances of family and race; an individual standing alone, self-reliant and self-propelling, ready to confront whatever awaited him with the aid of his own unique and inherent resources. . . . His moral position [is] prior to experience, and in his very newness he [is] fundamentally innocent."[1] The difference, however, is that the moral position of Hoffman's protagonists is *after* or *beyond* experience, what William Blake, in his understanding of man's development, described as a higher innocence whose achievement is only possible after a fall into experience, a movement beyond childhood naïveté into an innocence made possible by but which nevertheless transcends experience. Thus, having portrayed in earlier stories the wasteland into which modern southerners have fallen—not so much the Fugitive sense of an Eden paved over by business and industry as Milton's spiritual depiction of Paradise lost—it is as if Hoffman now offers to show the way back: Paradise regained. The collection's imperative, to *follow me home,* connotes as much, and what Hoffman clearly and quietly reveals in story after story is that home is where the heart lies. Redemption is there, the end of exile, peace. Only in "Night Sport," the earliest written of the stories, does Hoffman create a figure who again resembles Cain, a character motivated, like Gormer, Roy, and Dave, by selfishness.

Hoffman's fictional development from characters whose lives reflect a southern wasteland to those whose ethics redeem Jericho has biographical origins. Like R. W. B. Lewis, who as a major in the army surveyed the distant shores of the United States from the destruction of postwar Europe, detecting an American character type, Adam in a New World, Hoffman similarly discerned differences in the two cultures. Having participated in the invasion of Europe three days after Normandy, he witnessed the brutality and bloodshed as part of the Ninety-first Evacuation Hospital. Recently he recalled his impressions of the fighting, characterizing his mental understanding then as "a state of mind when everything was seen as destructible. Nothing stood firmly. Everything in life could equally vanish to no purpose,"

---

1. R. W. B. Lewis, *The American Adam: Innocence, Tragedy, and Tradition in the Nineteenth Century* (Chicago: University of Chicago Press, 1955), 5.

adding, "I did recognize that theirs was a culture different, much different, from ours, especially in art." Discharged in December 1945, Hoffman lacked any sense of self-value, feeling only the need to survive and often aroused to a fanatical response by even the slightest cause. Later, he declares, when he revisited Europe in 1949, courage and self-identity arrived, and he recognized that "the most impressive monuments we have are words."[2] Just as the juxtaposition of America and the Old World enabled Lewis to glean a distinctive personality in this country's literature, so too did this counterpoint offer Hoffman a sense of character understanding, not simply with respect to his own fictional protagonists but with himself as well.

What Hoffman insists upon in *Follow Me Home* is acceptance of what one may only call spirituality, a code of conduct or weltanschauung centered not on religion so much as on the realization that in the modern world all are wounded, lost, vulnerable. Consequently, what is required are the old-fashioned virtues of love, compassion, piety, humility, selflessness, and self-sacrifice. Through the thoughts, characteristics, and actions of the figure that Henry James labeled the center of revelation, Hoffman himself offers to show the reader in his eleven stories how to return home, echoing the words of the narrator in Robert Frost's poem "Directive":

> And if you're lost enough to find yourself
> By now, pull in your ladder road behind you
> And put up CLOSED to all but me.
> Then make yourself at home. . . .
>
> .   .   .   .
>
> Here are your waters and your watering place.
> Drink and be whole again beyond confusion.[3]

The journey involves women and men freed from the past (*emancipated* is Lewis's term) whose independence and self-reliance set them apart from the society around them and whose innocence, while not prior to experience (in a fallen world, that is not possible), derives from the inner realm of the heart. They often become childlike, with a simplicity or perhaps clarity of mind and thought that involves a "newness" of self.

2. William Hoffman, telephone interview by author, July 12, 1998.
3. *Selected Poems of Robert Frost* (New York: Holt, Rinehart and Winston, 1963), 251–53.

Generally speaking, the Hoffman hero is representative of American diversity. Of the eleven stories in *Follow Me Home,* four feature women, one of whom is African American, and while the monied aristocracy perhaps most evidences itself, the lower and middle classes also have their protagonists. Gender and economic status, in other words, have nothing to do in Hoffman's vision with finding the way home from the wasteland. Indeed, business acumen and wealth often hinder the journey toward wholeness, and "feminine" sensitivity and common sense are often prerequisites. The collection's balanced perspective speaks to spiritual inclusiveness, not political correctness, the idea that whatever the journey's path, it begins and ends with the inner self rather than outward circumstance.

The American Adam qualities of the Hoffman hero are nowhere more apparent than in Lizzie, in "Dancer," and Rachel, in "The Secret Garden."[4] Both women have figuratively left an old world whose attitudes and standards they believe inappropriate or insufficient in order to live among new values by which they define themselves. It is not that they follow Frost's less-traveled path; instead, they pursue a geography completely of their own making. Lizzie, for example, lives by herself in a small farmhouse that has been the "family place" (1) for five generations. She keeps its unused rooms neat and sequesters herself in the kitchen on winter days when the Virginia sun offers little warmth. Self-sufficient, she stubbornly clings to her independence, unwilling to accept visits from the Methodist preacher or assistance from her sister Mary Belle and brother-in-law Chester. Lizzie occasionally hears music, a fox-trot or waltz whose sounds reach her in spite of or through the wind, and when they do, she imaginatively dances with her arms around Oliver, her dead husband, a city-bred man who took to farming. Though he could not plow a straight furrow, he "dance[d] like a god . . . [and] knew how to make a lady feel she floated on air" (12). When Mary Belle discovers Lizzie dancing in her long johns, sweat shirt, and slippers during a snow-

4. Lewis, in *The American Adam,* argues that in a Bible-reading generation the hero was not surprisingly "most easily identified with Adam before the Fall. Adam was the first, the archetypal, man" (5). His study centers primarily on nineteenth-century American literature, including writers such as Whitman, the elder Henry James, Brown, Cooper, Hawthorne, and Melville. His focus consequently offers no opportunity for discussing what I call the American Eve. In discussing Hoffman's protagonists, I have continued to use Lewis's original term regardless of the gender of these main figures, believing that their principal characteristics remain the same.

storm, she brings her to Richmond, believing that the comfort her
wealth assures will be healthy for her. In such seeming opulence,
however, Lizzie withers; she is "accustomed to space and air" (8).
The guest rooms, painted "piggy pink" with pictures of "southern
belles and hat doffing cavaliers" (8); the master bedroom, "baby blue
with white flounces everywhere" (8); and the dining room, with its
long table and Williamsburg chandelier, all suffocate her independence and constitute a wasteland of richness that oppresses her
inner world, where music swells. "No use attempting to explain how
the music came and went," she thinks, "the sound nothing like violins
or saxophones but chiefly a feeling, if you could mix into melody the
smell of hay curing, the whisper of the river dragging under willow
branches, the taste of a freshly picked tomato still warm from the
sun, the sense of a good horse under you, the sight of a spiraling
hawk in a fresh summer sky, the touch of a loving man" (11). Only in
this element does Lizzie thrive.

The deaths of her husband and son years ago and the inability of
her sister to offer her a better life now leave Lizzie severed from all
family "inheritance." In her simplicity, Lizzie finds contentment, and
her independence and self-reliance sharpen her desire to confront life
with only her own resources. She desires no assistance, only freedom,
in whose music she touches life more closely than her sister and
brother-in-law, who "knew money, scented it like a bird dog winding"
(8). However, her self-sufficiency demands she escape the imposed in-
ternment. Two attempts fail, but when Lizzie one day recognizes the
full presence of spring and hears "a sea of music around her" (18), she
follows it, climbing a ladder left by the painters up to the roof. Her innocence renders her beyond experience, a woman whose childlike delight in the world is unsullied and complete: "As she looked up into
the limbs of a tulip poplar, she held out a palm to catch the slowly spiraling pollen" (18). When Lizzie, fearing that her sister will commit her
to a mental institution, follows the music onto the roof, the reader understands that, in the completeness of her imaginative world, Lizzie
achieves a spirituality that derives not from what was but from what
is, a wholeness that skeptics might label dangerous and delusional but
which Hoffman portrays as truly "home," a place in whose heights
Lizzie might breathe "fragrances filtered through a green veil of trees"
and where she feels "weightless" (19). That home, richer and newer
than any Mary Belle and Chester know, opens to her like spring, as
fresh and complete as Eden.

For Rachel, too, in "The Secret Garden," home becomes not a physical location but a spiritual state of mind. As with Lizzie, past events have conditioned the present, hastening her into a new geography whose inner landscape of moods reveals itself when she plays the piano. "I make a garden of quarter notes," she thinks, "I climb music as if it is a rose trellis reaching the sky" (180). Rachel has long ago abandoned the country of conventional morality, whose rigid standards mandate sexual propriety, the meaning of marriage, and the nature of personal giving. With her childish belief in love, she offers herself to men, a woman possessing "a heart too soon made glad" (188), though she realizes that they do not comprehend "the nature and completeness of my gift to them" (191). Certainly her husband has not understood what he believes to be her wantonness, her continual sexual offers to other men, and her inability to perceive the failure of their marriage. To his abiding concern about her affairs, she simply responds, "'We are all flowers, and they are beautiful children. . . . Who serves best, the bloom or the bee?'" (188). Indeed, her innocence most reflects itself in Rachel's identification with flowers. "I am a tea rose," she declares, "a purple iris, and often a long-stem tiger lily" (191). She knows, like an intuitive child, that "there are always gardens. . . . Women giv[ing] off nectar to the bees. It is so obviously a part of nature's plan you wonder why everyone doesn't see we are all gardens. I am the mimosa, and hummingbirds dart to me" (181). Rachel's romanticism lies not in her search for the spiritual in nature but rather in her belief that she herself is such an intimate part of the natural world. Despite the social, familial, and medical forces arrayed against her, all intent on altering who she is and how she acts, Rachel recognizes what they do not. "I have been chiefly a flower," she asserts. "It is the great truth I've perceived" (191).

Around the garden of herself lies a morass of southern manners and southern attitudes that admonish, scold, coerce, and guard. Her mother and children constantly observe her, returning behind Rachel's back the gifts she buys for others, and the doctors seek to curb or inhibit her behavior. Partly their actions derive from the perception of Rachel's emotional vulnerability and her physical unsteadiness, the "faint blue bruises on the elbows and forearms she used as fenders" (176), but they are also conscious of local gossip, the need to be discreet in a world whose wants and attitudes wither her bloom. Rachel senses their coldness, thinking, "Words are often wind. Pleas and threats. The first rule is never trust any wind. Voices speak of God" (181–82). Her innocence, which is beyond morality, lies in her motivation, her purity of thought, and her need for "my perfect little garden." That garden, with its biblical overtones of Eden, lies within herself, a mindscape where "wind cannot enter, my private place. Only a riot of blooms, the bees, the music" (182). Her independent behavior as well as her willingness to stand alone and to depend upon her own instincts and abilities sets her apart from the community. In the pristine climate of her private world, Rachel remains pure. Leaving family behind, she is undefiled by their inherited morality. Though "The Secret Garden" concludes with the family driving her north to a mental institution in Baltimore, Rachel remains undeterred, seeing upon her arrival not the "partially dark Victorian main building" but the flowers growing in front. In a story Hoffman structures by alternating perspectives, Rachel has the last word, "Coralbells" (193), she excitedly says, identifying the flowers, and in the play on words with "choral bells," Hoffman suggests her inner spirituality.

Hoffman balances Lizzie's and Rachel's monied backgrounds with his presentation of Celeste, the black cook of Miss Alice Louella in "Coals," and the unnamed narrator in "Boy Up a Tree," the sixteen-year-old daughter of a wealthy Tidewater aristocrat who learns more from the values of L. C. Spraggs, the lower-class son of a miner, than she does from the manners of her father. The two stories broaden Hoffman's depiction of the American Adam by effectively negating economic as well as gender qualifications while focusing on the character's emancipation from family, her self-reliance, and her innocence.

Celeste's independence lies in her determination to keep her word. As cook and caretaker of Miss Alice Louella, Celeste long ago promised the former's now-deceased husband that she would look after her. "'I give him my word'" (42), she asserts, and that frequently repeated declaration as well as her knowledge of human nature leads her not only to ignore the increasing requests of her dependent for "my tonic," the kind that made "birds fall out of trees" (42), but also to ban Raincoat, the man who surreptitiously brings the alcohol, from making his deliveries. Celeste, moreover, refuses to submit to the verbal harassment that Miss Alice Louella, whose late husband's wealth admitted him to the governor's patronage, is accustomed to using with her black help. When she admonishes Celeste, "'You continually try my patience,'" for example, the latter's response is direct and immediate: "'What patience?'" (43). Despite being first reprimanded and then released, Celeste remains untouched by monetary considerations, by the accepted role assigned to domestic help, and by her own family considerations. She has buried two of her previous husbands while refusing to live in the past.

Adherence to her verbal promise has only accentuated her self-reliance. Simply speaking, she does for herself, confronting whatever situation she meets with determination and her own abilities. That innate trust in who she is may be due partly to the physical disability of her present husband but more particularly to a fundamental faith in her beliefs. She is both practical and perceptive, able on the one hand to forgo her required uniform because her own dresses are cooler and on the other hand to negotiate a new business arrangement that pays her if Miss Alice Louella fires her again. Indeed, this new arrangement and the financial security it assures result in Celeste's assuming a moral position that elevates her from servant to protector. When Miss Alice Louella, angry and frustrated because Celeste requires her to leave her self-enforced isolation and return to the living, declares, "'You hate me, don't you?'" Celeste responds simply, "'I don't hate nobody. . . . Hate is sin'" (52). Celeste's care and concern are nothing less than love, a selfless expression of compassion. "'I nice not for what you has been but what you was and can be'" (54), she tells Miss Alice Louella; her love, which transcends economic considerations, not only causes her ward to rediscover a sense of vitality and purpose but also transforms Celeste into an individual whose spiritual innocence lies beyond the experiences that would otherwise cause bitterness and even hate. She remains morally pure, having long ago discovered and chartered a geography of the heart.

The unnamed narrator in "Boy Up a Tree" also learns from another individual, a teenaged boy from Cinder Hollow, where the inhabitants are "ridge-running hillbillies, mostly unschooled people who'd drifted down from the high country to find work in the mines" (81). However unlike "Coals," "Boy Up a Tree" centers less on how the narrator affects another as on how this outsider influences the main character, the young daughter of a Tidewater aristocrat who, in effect, reacts emotionally, physically, and psychologically to the other's actions and attitudes. Her decision to go out with L. C. Spraggs runs against the aristocratic traditions in which her parents have been raised and to which her father particularly adheres. "Gratitude has limits," he admonishes his daughter. "'You have to be kind, but don't encourage relationships'" (87). His daughter, however, is less concerned with distinctions of class and ancestry than with what might simply be called manners, the fact that this poor, uneducated admirer so persistently places her before himself. She accepts a date with L. C. but later, shortly before she attends boarding school, he distances himself from her out of shame. Only then does she recognize how important he is to her sense not only of herself but also of how life should be lived. Despite a parental injunction to "perpetuat[e] a tradition" (96), she follows another path within her heart, one more independent and leading to newer understandings, deeper truths. "Homesick among the blue bloods" (96) of her new school, she figuratively reaches out to him and sees his face, "like looking back," she thinks, "into a dark tunnel you're leaving and know you'll never return to" (97). Though she comprehends they will no longer meet, her willingness to abandon family, including the class traditions to which it subscribes, as well as her stand against economic prejudice, creates in her a simple, moral goodness or purity of heart that effectively renders her, in its newness, innocent, a fact Hoffman reinforces when the reader learns at the end of the story that she lives in Cinderella, West Virginia.

Against this array of female protagonists, Hoffman establishes an equally diverse group of male characters who also exhibit the characteristics of the American Adam. Amos, in "Sweet Armageddon," and Harmon, in "Abide with Me," not only represent the lower classes but also continue Hoffman's interest in depicting figures whose obsessive religious beliefs alienate them from the larger community. Amos, for example, lives with his wife, Martha, in a dilapidated neighborhood threatened by crime. His fundamentalist attitudes have effectively precluded him from obtaining his own ministry. Having earlier in his life deliberately chosen not to pursue a path promising wealth and material possessions, Amos recognizes that he and his wife have "[a]ll their lives together . . . been sojourners" (57). Living in a rented residence whose broken furniture and poor heating seem to mock his years of devoted service, he now works for the reward of Christ's Second Coming, "a celestial conflagration": "He pictured the cataclysm, the rolling thunder and horrible lightning streaking down black corridors of the earth, the dazzling rapture in the heavens" (59). Ignored by those with money, the "world's victors" (74), as well as by the church, which believes he carries "spiritual contagion" (75), Amos principally survives on his small ministerial retirement check, abandoned by "a sick, facile society that had forgotten its roots" (75).

Though at times resentful, he is never jealous. His reward, he believes, is not of this world but a spiritual home whose richness surpasses any earthly feast.

Amos is literally "bereft of ancestry, untouched and undefiled by the usual inheritances of family and race." He and Martha never mention family, to whom they would not turn for financial assistance should relatives offer. Amos has long ago left behind those whose wealth blinds them to "the sacred inviolability of Scripture" (75). Their independence purifies his faith. His part-time work as an orderly in a nursing home and her job as a clerk in a florist shop enable him to persevere, propelled by his beliefs and the knowledge that "at last God collects His loving family" (78). Certainly, Amos believes himself morally superior, especially when he unexpectedly breakfasts with an old college friend, a banker whose money and three marriages mock Amos's own faith. Indeed, the simplicity by which Amos lives, his abiding love of Martha that acutely acknowledges what she has surrendered for him, and his innate trust in God's Word give Amos an innocence that does not so much involve his ignorance of the world's evil (indeed, he is very conscious of man's wantonness) as it does an inner purity and childlike belief in his Father. When he wakes the following morning to "a crimson glow" through the nailed window, he thinks again of Armageddon. Wondering if he hears a trumpet, he holds Martha's hand and lifts his other "as if offering her and himself skyward on his own agitated palm" (78). The act is instinctive, and Hoffman clearly suggests that their rich faith has brought them to an inner home as abundant in religious provision as Eden was in bodily sustenance.

That same faith evidences itself in "Abide with Me," when, during a serious operation, Harmon sees Christ in a vision. As he "teeter[s] over the black pit" and stares at "the foul dog of death," "Him" appears, and Harmon finds himself "floating to the light" (100). Subsequently, he fulfills a promise made at that time, creating a huge, stone face of Jesus on a mountaintop and then lighting it so that "He seemed suspended in the high darkness" (103). Like Celeste in "Coals," he believes it necessary to keep his word. "I always been proud of doing that" (103), he thinks. Though not as poor as Amos, Harmon and his wife, Glenna Anne, live frugally, and he remains just as determined to adhere to his beliefs, particularly when the hewn image increasingly becomes a source of social contention and ridicule. Against a minister who suggests the face "don't look like Our Lord and Savior" (104) and an unidentified telephone voice who warns, "'Don't want no blue-eyed Eye-talians 'round here'" (105), Harmon remains resolute, insisting that the image is what he saw. "'I made a real promise'" (104), he states, believing in his independence and innocence that he will overcome the increasing community distress. He pays the cost of a building permit and turns away the ministerial delegation that arrives at his house seeking to convince him to take the statue down, declaring, "'I don't mean disrespect, but I been brought up to keep my word. I couldn't sleep nights if I didn't'" (108). Harmon even incurs the additional cost of fencing off the image, posting a No Trespassing sign, and paying for a newspaper advertisement. When his wife asserts, "'It's not worth it,'" he responds simply, "'Never been a question of worth but of word'" (112). Complaints that the face is anti-Semitic and that it affronts feminist groups do not deter him, nor does he yield when offered fifteen hundred dollars by a private collector of folk art. Yet when local rowdies deface "Him" and use the area to drink, Harmon finally responds. He drives them off and then, almost apologetically, "cover[s] his eyes and bow[s] his head" (116), blasting the base of the image with dynamite he has stolen and burying the face in one of his wife's clean sheets. When the police arrive the next morning, he says to the deputy, "'I always believed it about the most important thing in the world for a man to keep his word'" (116).

Throughout the story, Harmon relies on his clarity of vision and on promises he has made, undeterred even when Glenna Anne expresses reservations that not so much abandon him as leave him free to confront the rigid community with his own abilities. He does so, using resources that effectively stand against southern narrow-mindedness. Only when he recognizes that he has kept his word and that taking the hewn stone down benefits "Him" does Harmon settle the issue by eliminating the cause. He is genuinely ignorant of the prejudice and political correctness that subvert a simple expression of private gratitude and spiritual love. "The first trouble he didn't suspect was trouble at all" (103), Hoffman writes, and while that lack of suspicion gradually yields to the expectation of problems, Harmon remains morally innocent, conscious of what a promise means, his spiritual position "beyond experience." As the police car takes him away from Glenna Anne, he never leaves the purer home that lies within his heart.

While Amos and Harmon center themselves with the spiritual, other protagonists live essentially within this world. Stories such as "Tides," "Points," and "Business Trip" portray protagonists searching for self who discover a revitalized future as they abandon old beliefs. They enter a new world either deliberately or unexpectedly, facing situations never before confronted and determined to accommodate themselves and persevere. Self-reliant, they are survivors. In "Tides," for example, Wilford and his son Dave are sailing for the last time before the latter begins a banking career following his college graduation. Dave refers to their Chesapeake Bay trip as "a ritual celebrating the official end of fun in my life" (20). A quiet man, Wilford also hopes to make the cruise a "celebration" (21), during which he might summon words of appreciation. When the boat, appropriately named *Wayfarer*, is commandeered by a criminal and forced to sail towards Baltimore, Wilford faces a dangerous dilemma, conscious that he must act but also that his own son has "never really been strong" (30). He fears for Dave and recognizes in the reminiscences he allows himself that their past together up until that morning has been safe: "He remembered how the night before he and Dave had lain on the cabin top and identified the Pleiades, Orion, and Andromeda. The sky had seemed benevolent" (31). The outside world, however, almost always forces itself upon Hoffman's protagonists, threatening to coil its contagion into the Edenic innocence.

As the boat sails to Baltimore, Wilford seems literally to free himself from history, leaving behind in the boat's wake all sense of security and safety. His past becomes irrelevant, everything dependent on what happens now. What Wilford discovers is not that he does not know how to act but that he is in danger of thinking too much, of "second-guessing himself into immobility" (35). With a silent prayer, "God, let me be brave this once" (37), he propels himself into action, relying on his own instincts when his son distracts their abductor into losing his balance; together they subdue the intruder. Dave loses a tooth in the struggle, but Wilford, temporarily suffering a loss of focused vision from a gunshot, more importantly surrenders his fear that Dave lacks manhood, that he is too soft. Wilford's decision always to keep the incisor his son has lost symbolically suggests his entrance into a new world, a realm where childhood and manhood are not magically determined by age and where he and Dave now share renewed bonds of trust and respect. Moreover, Wilford, though conscious of the evil that always threatens to intrude, nevertheless maintains a moral position above experience. He gratefully acknowledges his debt to all who have helped his son, including Dave's girlfriend: "The filling satisfaction to have him as he was now. Bless

Margaret too, Wilford thought, and lowered his head to the sand"
(22). His reverence is sincere, uncorrupted by selfishness.

Beau in "Points" and the unnamed narrator in "Business Trip" also
exhibit this reverence whose nature is essentially religious and
whose efficacy owes to the protagonist's fundamental innocence.
Although Hoffman's southern wasteland is sometimes physical, as a
result of industrialism and urban growth, it is more often a spiritual
corruption. In this view, moral innocence, while no longer a priori as
with Adam, nevertheless represents a general state or condition unsullied by selfishness and ego. Hoffman's protagonists possess a special attitude, a faith that resides in this world but is not of it. In
"Points," for example, Beau's belief in foxhunting is as pure and unre-
lenting as Lizzie's love of music, Rachel's identification with flowers,
or Amos's trust in the Second Coming. Prior to the hunt, he repeats a
silent prayer: "Let there . . . be no wind. Let the sun warm the earth,
yet not so faintly that the ground thaws only on top and remains
frozen inches beneath. Allow footing to be safe. Permit no jump ap-
proaches to become icy bogs horses slide and crash into. Let the fox
run straight and true" (139). Alive in its traditions, Beau does not so
much reside in the past as respond to the present southern emptiness, a recognition of evil and the assumption of a pure ideal. Beau
considers it "a statement of where one stood in respect to a world becoming increasingly common, disordered, and hateful" (139), which
is to say that he deliberately chooses a moral position that transcends experience while being conscious of it. In so doing, Beau
achieves a spiritual purity.

His choice creates divisiveness, and Hoffman clearly indicates that
with his present attitudes, Beau has separated himself from his family, a man now "untouched and undefiled by the usual inheritances."
He has divorced his first wife, whose infidelity and sarcasm insulted
his values, leaving her their house. His second divorce resulted from
that wife's miserliness, her unwillingness to enjoy life by spending
money even reasonably (she had requested he not flush the toilet unless absolutely necessary). Beau believes in what he terms "the art of
life" (146), the charm and beauty and fullness money permits, a
Fitzgerald-like attitude different from that of his son Alfred, who
thinks "of money only in terms of dollars, not the grace attached, the
concomitant manners" (146). While Beau understands that life expects a response, Alfred has "failed to grasp that living could be a
portrait in which a person was both subject and artist" (146). That
belief sustains and incites Beau to action during the foxhunt, a chase

during which he confronts modern degeneration and diminishment by relying on his abilities and instincts, a knowledge of when to act. When Clive, who overpowers his mounts and who preserves the fox's brush in Lucite, mounting it as a trophy, determines to keep the lead, Beau challenges him, believing the latter's egotism an affront to the gentility of his code of conduct. His trust in and use of his horse, Windlord, enable him to overtake Clive, ending the hunt with dignity and ritual, his independence and self-reliance affirmed.

The unnamed narrator in "Business Trip" possesses a code of ethics that echoes Beau's, and the two stories follow each other in the collection. His fundamental innocence lies partly in the reverence he holds for the game he and Harrison, his business partner, kill during their seasonal hunting trips to the West Virginia cabin they themselves have built. The sparse accommodations and their reverential conduct constitute "our shrine to the ruffed grouse" (157). They impose on themselves a spartan regimen intended to ensure they remain "as unencumbered and untainted as possible by lowland civilization" (157). However, the surprise the narrator receives at the story's conclusion where, despite his business acumen, he only later realizes that Clarence, an invited guest, has duped him, also suggests his ignorance of social evil and duplicity.

Hoffman's protagonist most reveals an Adamic self-reliance in his efforts to keep out civilization. Though he is no Thoreau or Natty Bumppo, both because his endeavors are not solitary but in collaboration with those of his partner and because his errands into the wilderness are an escape rather than a mission, he nevertheless determines to create a refuge that constitutes a return to a more basic, even primitive life. In his efforts to clear the land, build a cabin (including a chimney with stones lifted and hauled from a stream), and limit the influence or encroachment of civilization, the protagonist exhibits a self-propelling independence, a willingness to confront nature on its own terms with only his own resources. It is a philosophy toward life that reveals itself in an almost Hemingwayesque code of conduct. The rituals that the narrator follows, particularly when hunting, clearly indicate a ruggedness whose prototype lies in frontiersmen such as Davy Crockett and Daniel Boone. He believes, simply stated, that there is "joy in adversity" and that "in the high country truth prevailed" (158).

Entering that high country, the narrator leaves behind family, specifically his wife, Trixie, and his emancipation is significant in that she epitomizes all that he does not: "She was high style—tall, eyes dark, her stride sure. She carried a gloss. She liked the money" (158). The protagonist also likes success, but the cabin demands a different behavior, an alternative set of sustaining values that are also concrete. Good liquor is to be honored with glasses, for example, and a grouse killed is celebrated by not wasting the meat. When Clarence, who is Trixie's boss, feigns outdoor ineptness and then reveals his proficient marksmanship, the narrator wonders at his motivation for remaining secretive. His wonder becomes genuine terror when Clarence's furtive comments imply that Trixie would be better off with him, financially and emotionally, and when Clarence's gait continually swings his Browning rifle toward him. The possibility that Clarence seeks to kill him, claim an accident, and then have Trixie and the insurance money causes the protagonist to flee. He falls, bloodies his head, and wets his pants, while Clarence laughs and yells to Harrison, "'Look what I discovered!'" (175). Hoffman never indicates Clarence's true intent, but the fact that the narrator believes the implied threat real indicates not only his essential innocence despite his worldliness but that the outside world continues to be dangerous, inhabited by individuals whose avarice or egotism creates a wasteland that Hoffman's Adamic figures must acknowledge or confront.

"Night Sport," published in the October 1986 issue of the *Atlantic,* is the oldest story in *Follow Me Home,* and its darkly pessimistic narrative and black tone link the collection to Hoffman's earlier stories. Its inclusion in this most recent grouping of stories serves to underscore Hoffman's development from a perspective almost rigidly Calvinistic in its bleak assessment of human nature to one more balanced and even affirmative in its depiction of human triumphs, the small victories that confront life's larger diminishments and defeats. It presents a narrator whose Adamic qualities conceal a fundamental delight in imparting pain to others—an ironic reversal of the Christian principle that it is better to give than receive. Chip is a Vietnam veteran who lost his legs in an Asian jungle and who now insists upon his independence by buying a small frame house in "the western boonies of the county" (124). Despite his Electroped and two sets of legs—compliments of the Veterans Administration and the "prosthetic miracles of American ingenuity" (120)—he remains darkly bitter. With senses honed by combat, he feels the slightest vibration inside his "frame typee" (124) and senses the passage of a dung beetle through humid leaf mold, its scratchings as "loud as a scream" (120). He knows a truth, he believes, revealed in "the absolute brilliance which exploded not from outside but within—a white fire so searing and almighty it cauterized him clean" (122). Chip meets all offers of help or sympathy with abrasive sarcasm as intense as any comment by, say, Mr. Gormer in "The Spirit in Me." Indeed, the knowledge he owns is religious, deep and abiding and irrevocable.

His independence, moreover, involves leaving family behind, "happily bereft" (5) in his freedom not only from the wealth and cultural leisure of his parents, whose aristocratic background irritates him, but also from what he considers their intrusiveness. He has developed, literally and figuratively, "a sense of darkness" (117) into which others cannot see and from which he appears incapable of returning. With his Maytag to assure his cleanliness and a supply of basic provisions, he lives "on automatic alert" (120), psychologically prepared to inflict physical damage on someone—anyone—whom he has tricked into entering his deliberately unlit, seemingly deserted house. Only in their pain and disfigurement can Chip feel alive. Therefore, when Thomas Walker, a boy whose name subconsciously fuels Chip's hatred, breaks into his house as part of an initiation into a private school club, Chip pretends to let him leave, only to fire both barrels of the rifle into the youth's calves when he suddenly believes Walker feels sorry for him. He thinks, "they ought to have to learn. They needed to know" (134). As he dials the police to inform them he has shot an intruder, Chip delights in the boy's new understanding, almost reveling as "the terrible knowledge, the deepest knowledge of all, flowed into those honey-brown eyes" (135). His moral position is never prior to experience but altogether outside it, his spiritual state beyond good and evil and therefore, ironically, beyond all such morality. Chip not only aligns himself with earlier characters like Gormer, Ray, and Dave, but in so doing reminds the reader of a larger truth. In the southern wasteland, whose expanse causes Chip, when he looks through his unwashed windows and sees "dirt either way" (124), the city of Richmond "oozing" west with a corruption that "devoured field and forest" (117), live characters whose Adamic qualities do not promise a paradise revisited, the way home, but a reaffirmation of its loss.

Chip's inclusion in *Follow Me Home* underscores another aspect of the American experience delineated by Lewis in his seminal study. Noting that "[t]he dismissal of the past has only been too effective" (9), Lewis issues a warning manifested by American literature. To ignore the past, he argues, is to repeat it. "We regularly return," Lewis declares, "decade after decade and with the same pain and amaze-

ment, to all the old conflicts, programs, and discoveries" (9). In link-
ing Chip to earlier protagonists warped by self-centeredness and a
debilitating resentment, Hoffman not only shows where Americans in
general and southerners in particular have gone but also how we
might once again become lost.

Yet the final statement of *Follow Me Home* is decidedly optimistic,
a declaration that we need not repeat the past in our ignorance or for-
getfulness of it but reclaim and replenish what we once were. In
"Expiation," the collection's last story, Hoffman presents Leland and
his wife, Anne, who, after leaving their daughter at an elite, private
women's college for her senior year, travel "roads little changed from
the time way back" (194) to visit his southern boyhood heritage. A
successful businessman who long ago moved to the North, Leland allows memories of his youth to unfold around him as he drives past
fields grown wild with thistle and crumbling buildings covered with
creeper, honeysuckle, and poison oak. Anne becomes increasingly unsettled at the decay she observes everywhere; familiar with wealth,
she expects a South idealized by her husband's images of magnolias
and dogwoods lining the paved road to a white plantation. "'So few
houses'" (198), she says, and when the asphalt yields to hard-packed
red clay, she nervously asks, "'You're certain this is the way, you're
not lost?'" (206). Leland, however, understands that he is only now
finding himself. Having misled his wife for years about his childhood,
allowing her to imagine "visions of past status and grandeur" (209), he
courageously confronts who he was—a poor sharecropper's son who
ate possum and groundhog and who was once sent home from school
with head lice.

Having lived for years in "Yankeeland" (211), his parents long dead,
his past long closed to him, Leland remains "untouched and undefiled by the usual inheritances of family and race." As he meets the
caretaker of the manor for which his father worked and that a timber
company presently owns, he remembers the owner's second wife, a
rich, pretty northerner who took him riding one day, the horse so fast
he learned *"what flying is like"* (207). More importantly, he understands not only the selfless generosity of her gift but also that his denial of the past demands a present atonement. When he sees a poor
black "[t]ripping" (212), trying to leave the sun-baked county he himself had abandoned, his vision becomes larger: "he pictured youths
leaving, all over the world, hundreds, thousands headed down alien
roads to find what waited at the end. He saw himself" (212). Though

he knows his wife, shocked and angered at his years of deception and fearful now of all blacks, will "punish him, make him pay" (213), he acts independently, writing the youth, whose fully packed car has broken down, a traveler's check. As their Cadillac prepares to enter the junction that will lead them back to the interstate and "the other life" (213), Leland once again looks backward, alone in his determination, and notices "wildly flourishing trumpet vines" and "strands of rusted, broken barbed wire" (213), symbols of natural hope and failed human dreams that together represent the continuity of life.

Hoping their marriage will withstand the breach caused by "a good lie well intended" (211), Leland for the first time reconciles himself with his own past and prepares for what will now come, "fundamentally innocent," as Lewis writes, "in his very newness" (5). The generous and spontaneous actions that move him backward in time while helping another social outcast travel forward become an ethic of personal redemption, enabling him to discover a new geography. It is a land he recognizes as home, that most necessary of places long forgotten in the crass materialism of the southern wasteland, having recovered it by driving over "uneven ground . . . down the road once forbidden" (209). Although the caretaker tells Leland, "'All the people who was around here is gone. They all gone'" (210), he is wrong, quite wrong. William Hoffman has never left this realm of the human heart, knowing that the journey there is as much spiritual as physical. His stories are a directive mapping the way home. The reader need only follow.

"To Cause No One Pain"

The Ethical Imperative in William Hoffman's Literature

Ron Buchanan

William Hoffman is a consummate storyteller, creating intriguing plots that engross the reader with diabolical twists and counterpoints. His well-wrought tales, though, are merely vehicles for his characters, the true basis for his narrative strength and reputation, as he constantly creates figures entangled in moral destruction. His protagonists are tragic heroes in the classical sense, undergoing the entire development sequence outlined by Aristotle in his *Poetics* some twenty-four hundred years ago. Repeatedly, their tragic flaw is that they suffer from positive values waylaid in contemporary society, and thus they are doomed because of their loyalty to and faith in those values. Hoffman has expressed this paradox in the succinct ethical imperative "cause no one pain." Originally stating this moral principle in the reworked first manuscript that became his second published novel, *Days in the Yellow Leaf,* Hoffman has repeated this idea explicitly or implicitly throughout his novels and short stories.

Hoffman's edict produces a moral dilemma. When he argues that persons should avoid hurting others—either physically, psychologically, emotionally, or circumstantially—he forces his characters into a no-win code of conduct that alienates them from others. By adopting such a code, the protagonists become passive, avoiding the grittiness of life, and thus they suffer the cruelest injustice of all: by causing no one else pain, they themselves suffer for their conduct. Thus, we find an ironic moral viewpoint with two mutually exclusive results. One possibility is for the protagonists to be integral parts of life's activities and the ensuing difficulties that stem from various situations and relationships. Alternatively, they can distance themselves from life and avoid any confrontational situations, thereby ensuring that they will cause themselves grief and guilt and physical pain. Even though he promotes this interrelationship tenet as the guiding principle for our dealings with other people, Hoffman ultimately realizes that the result will be disastrous for any who practice it. Still, his message is that life's purpose is in the journey, not in the destination, and he preaches his no-pain concept as the road map for our trip. Such a position is not naive, nor is it innocent. Hoffman's characters eventually realize that they live in worlds fraught with circumstances they cannot control. While they can, at best, structure their own activities, they cannot control the myriad factors that merely living inflicts upon their lives, just as they cannot control the prices the hardware store charges its customers, the wages an employer pays his workers, or the number of beers the driver of the car approaching them on the highway has consumed. And yet, each action influences their dealings with those individuals. While the protagonists can conscientiously avoid inflicting any further pain upon these persons through inaction, they eventually find themselves entrapped by that inaction in circumstances that create hardships they cannot avoid. What they ultimately come to, then, is an epiphany that they must use Hoffman's edict as one tool for creating order from the chaotic circumstances of their lives and finding some sort of significance in the act of enduring their own pain.

Days in the Yellow Leaf is an appropriate illustration of Hoffman's philosophy. He takes the title from the second verse of George Gordon, Lord Byron's poem, "On This Day I Complete My Thirty-sixth Year": "My days are in the yellow leaf; / The flowers and fruits of Love are gone; / The worm, the canker, and the grief / Are mine alone!" (5–8). The poem as a whole is a realization of lost ideals and youthful ambitions and innocence, ending with a death wish in glorious battle as the only plausible recourse for such despair. Hoffman carries this gloom into the novel, set in West Virginia shortly after World War II, through his central character, Tod Young, a recently married veteran and son of a bank president. As we first encounter young Tod, he has unwillingly taken on the trappings of conventional society; he has married Grace Sand because "she needed him" (82), and he has just accepted a menial position at his father's bank because "he had spent a lot of time trying to think of something else he could do. There was simply nothing else" (11).

It has taken Tod some two years of civilian life to reach this stage of his life, and immediately the reader sees Tod ensnared by circumstances that force him to participate in the realities of life. Shamed by his father for registering as a conscientious objector, Tod had eventually enlisted in the army and had earned "quite a reputation as a killer":

> The other men thought he liked to kill, but each time, the shame went all the way through him. Caring nothing for his own life, he would volunteer for anything. On the nights there were no

> patrols he would slip out with a knife. During one rainy night he
> got seven. He had received a letter that day from his father telling
> him how proud he was that Tod was facing up.
>   He didn't want any medals. All he wanted was to die, and he
> thought that would be easy with so much death around. (101)

This passage points out one of the major conflicts in the novel, the intense destructive relationship between Will Young, the macho hunter and self-made bank president father, and Tod Young, the sensitive and pacifistic son defiantly trying to assert his independence. By being a conscientious objector, Tod declares his uneasiness with killing, the result of the many hunting trips Will has forced Tod to take with him, but Will, stung by his son's unmanliness, has inflicted such emotional and psychological pain upon Tod because of the declaration that the young man can no longer resist. Tod therefore abandons his principle and enlists, but he uses the war as a means to escape his own pain, hopefully by achieving the very death wish Byron espouses in the closing of his poem: "Seek out—less often sought than found— / A soldier's grave, for the best; / Then look around, and choose thy ground, / And take thy rest" (37–40). Thwarted in his plans, Tod returns home a hero, but because of the conflict between his war experiences and his moral imperative, he cannot easily readjust and exhibits many of the characteristics of the lost generation returning from World War I, feeling "very tired" and "as if he were a long way off. It was as if there was nothing inside him looking out" (60). Partially as atonement for the killing and partially as a reaffirmation of his earlier philosophy, Tod now emphatically embraces a nonviolent approach to life, refusing even to defend himself as a poolroom bully repeatedly slaps him in an effort to provoke a fight.

Tod Young continues his search for a meaningful existence although previously he had been unable to complete his studies for the ministry and had been disheartened by articles he proofread for the newspaper. He finally begins to experience some semblance of idyllic life through his marriage to Grace Sands and his work at the bank. Tod has used his philosophy as an ethical guide to create order from the chaos of life with his father and the war and its aftermath. As he assumes greater responsibility at the rigid, insensate bank and as he and Grace prepare for their coming baby in their new house on the correct side of the mountain, Tod believes he has been able to integrate his peaceful existence with the interactive demands of life:

Suddenly it occurred to Tod he was completely happy. No matter how he looked at it, for once everything seemed to be going
right. He understood that this was a rare moment for him and
wanted to hold onto it as long as possible. There were bound to
be times ahead when things would all seem wrong. In those times
he would try to remember this.

Then another thought occurred to him. As far as he knew, he
had achieved the moment without hurting anyone, at least without hurting them badly. (138)

Tod has taken on the "materialistic" elements of society—wife, home,
job—and still maintained a harmonious distance from the hurtful exi-
gencies those elements entail. But the closing line of that passage
forces Tod to realize that, despite his best efforts, he has caused pain,
maybe not physical pain but assuredly a disturbing pain. Yet he believes that the pain, however slight, that he has caused—to his father,
to his wife, to his war buddies—is bearable and has caused no ir-
reparable damage.

Tod's life has reached its zenith. He has been unable to fulfill his
death wish and has reentered the social realm of his life, even if only
on a superficial level. He has attempted to bridge the idealistic and
realistic aspects of that reintegration while accumulating the signs of
an apparently successful participation in that life. From this point,
Tod's world begins to disintegrate.

Grace feels that Tod lacks the ruthlessness to take control of business and be enormously successful in their social environment, and
that he would thus deprive her of her dream lifestyle. She chastises
him as weak and ineffectual, especially after he quits his bank position to take a sales job. When she miscarries, Grace blames Tod for
his insistence that they abandon the country-club lifestyle of an eventual bank president, including the new house Will had given them as
a wedding present. In a further effort to hurt Tod, Grace seduces his
best friend, Grant Wolfe, planning the liaison for the hour when Tod
would return to their walk-up flat for lunch. When he sees the two
most important people in his life engaged in a sexual act, Tod uses
the shotgun he had carried on the hunting trips with his father to kill
the two. Will pays off the judge, the prosecutor, and the governor in
order to acquit his son of murder charges, but doing so means that
the conspiracy must show Grant Wolfe as a depraved sex fiend rather
than the protective, helpful realist he has always been toward Tod.
Acquitting Tod also means presenting Grace as a helpless victim

rather than the embittered, manipulative shrew she had become. Will Young's efforts to save his son cause Tod to face his guilt, which is born of pain caused to others, and he immediately turns the guilt upon himself, the perpetrator.

To underscore the thematic relationships among his characters, Hoffman uses symbolism, especially through the characters' names: "I use names to suggest themes, ideas. I do not use symbols for symbolism's sake, but to buttress, to strengthen what I'm trying to say."[1] "Tod Young" is the product of the German word for "death" and an English adjective that suggests immaturity and ongoing development. Thus Tod exhibits his youthful death wish, reinforced through his name, but the name also suggests his stage of development as moving from malaise and disenfranchisement to endurance and involvement in life. Note also that Will Young's name recalls his strong determination as a self-made businessman, but it also indicates his growing and maturing relationship with his son. In contrast to the pervasive gloom of Byron's poem, *Days in the Yellow Leaf* will end with a more optimistic outlook on the relationship between the father and the son. Similarly, Grace Sands's first name reminds us of her delicacy and search for a cultured lifestyle. Her last name, though, underscores the unstable, shifting nature of her personality as she becomes shrewish and manipulative. Grant Wolfe's name aligns him with Grace through their alliterative first names, his recalling a suave and debonair entertainment personality (Cary Grant) and a deliberative and successful military figure (U. S. Grant). His last name recalls the literal predatory elements of a wolf, reminding us again of Tod's wartime exploits and basis for the young men's friendship, while simultaneously reminding us of the term's colloquial use describing a rabid seducer. In these examples and throughout his works, Hoffman uses symbolism to underscore personalities, ironically emphasizing or contrasting his integral themes.

The lies required to acquit Tod of murder create further tension between father and son, and they prompt Tod to cry out during the trial about the injustice being perpetrated upon him and his victims. Having killed two people, Tod again pronounces his death wish: "'Don't you see what I did. I don't want to be saved'" (301). Tod's real punishment thus becomes his having to live with his guilt rather than

1. William Hoffman, interview with the author, Longwood College, Farmville, Va., spring 1980.

receiving an appropriate death sentence, which would end for him any suffering he would have to face. Again thwarted by circumstances he cannot control, Tod faces the ignominy of an acquittal and must once again reinstate himself as part of his social world. His deflated morality, utterly shattered by his violent act during a nonviolent period of his life, now precludes any sense of superiority. A suicide attempt interrupted by his father is the final crushing defeat, and Tod begs forgiveness, to which Will Young replies, "'A father doesn't have to forgive his son anything'" (353). Both men have now reached a spiritual union where they can understand the other's extreme nature. This position will allow them to cause each other no more affective pain.

Taking Will Young's statement about a father not needing to forgive a son to a religious symbolic level—that it parallels a deity's forgiveness of the worshiper—is an idea not without merit within the context of Hoffman's imperative to cause no one pain. Sin and its associated guilt can cause the wrongdoer pain on an emotional level, yet knowledge of forgiveness eases that pain. And, while much of his work focuses on the physical pain related to injury, death, or both, Hoffman is also concerned with the emotional anguish of sin and guilt.

Consider Hoffman's novel *A Walk to the River,* in which a small-town Virginia minister, Paul Elgin, would rather suffer the shame of being ousted from his pulpit because of an unjust accusation that he attacked Caroline Gaines, the wife of a prominent local businessman, than admit publicly that he had known her as the local tramp in his college town. Caroline's guilt—and thus her own pain caused merely by Paul's presence in the Black Leaf community—about her self-acknowledged misdeeds can be assuaged only by the minister's sacrifice. Caroline relies on superficial attributes such as her social position to remake her identity and contemptuously forces Paul to yield to her; although he has undergone a more substantial conversion of values, Paul understands that his revelations about Caroline's past will destroy not only her family but also the townspeople who believe both in Caroline's basic goodness and in their minister's obvious baseness. Although he is desperate to protect himself and his family, Paul will not recount Caroline's past, but he vainly hopes that she will confess her "sins" and thus save the principals concerned, he physically and she morally.

Just before the church meeting at which Paul's ecclesiastical fate will be determined, Jackson LeJohn, chairman of the church's board of officers and the novel's narrator, confronts Paul with the evidence he has discovered about the minister and Caroline; the two men discuss briefly Paul's planned defense:

> "Don't give them Caroline," I said.
> He frowned.
> "I've protected her," he said. "Who could have done more for her than I have?"
> "I think that means you'll throw her to them."
> "If I can, I'll shield her," he said angrily. "But I have my family and work to think of." (297)

Paul ultimately realizes that he will have to reveal Caroline's past as Rosy Mice if he is to save himself, and he is about to make public her background when Caroline walks into the church with her two daughters: "Paul backed away as if from fire. He shook his head. He saw the truth in the flesh. If he saved himself, or a part of himself, he would have to ruin other human beings. He would have to offer them up" (317).

Herein lies the core of Paul's dilemma of causing no pain: If he himself is to avoid the pain associated with his ouster, he must cause the pain of humiliation to another. Pain, in this case moral and emotional, is an integral part of life, the catalyst that establishes decorum and civility between persons. Both as a human being and as a minister, Paul becomes the scapegoat assuming the sins of his congregation and friends. Having repudiated his own sinful, debauched past, Paul has undergone a conversion experience—much like St. Paul—and as the unblemished, guileless, and innocent substitute for his own flock, the thought of "giving up" Caroline is as repugnant to him as is the very possibility that he could have attacked her.

This novel seems to end on a negative note. A righteous minister has been sacrificed to appease one loudmouthed town bully and his madeover wife's reputation. The protagonist and narrator, Jackson LeJohn, has succeeded in his charge of discovering the truth about the backgrounds of Paul Elgin and Caroline Gaines, but he has given up a good man in favor of maintaining the sham existence of two lesser, though wealthier, citizens. Jackson, a widower, has even lost his "young and modern" summertime girlfriend, Val, because of her disgust with the citizens' gloating over the minister's ouster and her realization that Jackson will never overcome his wife's death (330–31). He has even lost his twelve-year-old son to the adult world of big business as the youngster attempts to implement the business practices and ethics of chain hardware stores at LeJohn's independent, family-based store. And yet, the final paragraph notes Jackson's recognition of the lesson Paul Elgin had realized many years earlier, just before his conversion: "I bit down on my sadness. I thought that even pain had goodness. A dead man couldn't suffer. To grieve, a man had to be alive and to care about something" (336). Jackson realizes that pain is mankind's link to living, that without pain people are at best walking shells, unresponsive and callous. The ability "to care about something" brings people into the brotherhood of humanity where they must interact and therefore risk pain. Jackson acknowledges his role in the congregation's "trial" and his failure to prevent Paul's departure. He faces his intense devotion to his departed wife and his inability to truly love Val. While he cannot resist these forces, he can attempt to retrieve those elements of his life still available to him, so he devotes more attention to his son's childhood and settles for a friendly relationship with Val.

Jackson LeJohn's situation parallels Tod Young's in that both men destroy a man and a woman that they care about. Their situations differ, however, in that Jackson's behavior results from his trying to distance himself from life and merely go through the motions of living, while Tod's actions result from an effort to be a vital part of the social community. The end result in each case is similar, though, as the pain each man endures helps him make sense of his life and determine the course he will follow.

Although acknowledged for his novels, Hoffman works far better in the tighter, more succinct realm of short stories, which often continue his philosophy of causing no pain, but frequently the lessons to be learned from the stories are lessons of manners. In many of these stories, Hoffman shows his readers the polite and genteel interactions necessary to maintain a daily existence while enduring life's ugliness. Many of these tales center on conflicts between men and women, at least one of whom is frequently a widow or widower, and the stories often turn on one character's begrudging politeness toward and acceptance of the other. Two suitable examples of such stories are "Altarpiece," which was reprinted in *By Land, by Sea,* and "Doors," the title story of Hoffman's 1999 collection.

In "Altarpiece," Peck wants nothing more than to rid himself of the physical mementos of his late wife and to sell their century-old Cumberland County farmhouse. His plan is to insulate himself from others in the family's summer cottage on the Chesapeake Bay and there submit himself to a quasi-suicidal isolation with his memories of Kate. His strategy falls apart, though, when Jenny Coates thrusts herself into his reticent existence. A door-to-door cosmetics salesperson, Jenny has spent her family fortune and income "'putting on the dog. No woman's man was safe while she was on the loose'" (133). Her three marriages have left her destitute financially and nearly as bankrupt emotionally, but she possesses a determination that forces her into the lives of her customers and community. Harassed constantly by financial problems and by a combative, trashy daughter, Jenny senses in Peck someone as much in need of love as she, and she will not abandon him in his time of despair.

She frequently drops by with a loaf of fresh-baked bread, but when Jenny does not appear for several weeks, he becomes concerned and discovers that "'[t]here have been reverses'" that have forced her to give up her small house and move into a smaller cottage (138). During the coming months their relationship develops into one of mutual companionship until the night Jenny passionately kisses Peck, at which point he jerks back in fright and she locks herself in her cottage. Looking through her window, Peck sees Jenny crying on the bed: "He'd never witnessed such sorrow, not even in himself—a pain that wrenched and shrank her body. She flinched as if being flogged. Her mouth's wail was soundless through the beaded window. Her suffering, he believed, came not from him alone. Rather, his rejection of her on the porch had been but the last step down a pitiless slope to a final, all-conquering despair" (142).

Peck's epiphany about Jenny's motives moves him to comfort her. "'Whom grief has joined . . . '" his mind repeats as he overtly attempts to assuage the hurt he has caused (143). Differences of class and attitudes no longer matter as the two people support each other, she bringing him back from indolence and he bringing her back from exaggerated dejection. Peck recognizes the emotional bond between them to be significant because "they shared great sadnesses: the fellowship of grief" (139). Two incomplete beings, they together become one complete couple who "inflict no pain on each other—pangs of living that like the rain fall on the just and unjust alike" (139). In this case, the grief, deserved or not, that each person endures separately eases the pain of both as long as they remain polite to each other. In the process, they find together a love that grows stronger through the fire of grief. Like Jackson LeJohn, Peck discovers that pain is the sign of a person's affirmation of life, that the very mortality he and

Jenny enjoy can be real only in their search for some dignity amidst the many difficulties they encounter.

Whereas Peck and Jenny build a relationship on mutual pain, in the short story "Doors" the main character, the widow Flora, establishes a relationship based on respect as she hires Tobaccoton's best handyman, Horace Puckett, to repair her house. Like Peck, Flora is a member of the community's gentry, and like Jenny, Horace—called Horace Horsecollar by Flora—is part of the county's menial working class. More separates Flora and Horace than merely dollars, yet she has difficulty understanding that more unites them than merely the old furnace and radiators the proud Flora wishes to have Horace maintain yearly, although he refuses: "'Nope. . . . I work for people who think I'm good enough to be invited inside. You wouldn't even have me up to eat my soup and sandwich. I'm making out your bill here, which comes to forty dollars. It'd been less if you hadn't made me feel I smelled like a wet dog. . . . I wouldn't've come in your house. I just expected to be treated respectful'" (6–7). Horace expresses his own sense of pride as he chastens Flora for her ill manners. Like William Faulkner's many yeoman farmers, Horace has a simple ethic of hard work, fair prices, and due respect for one's talents and obligations. But Horace's directness about his "ridiculous feelings" offends Flora's gentility even as she fears needing his services again.

Flora soon learns of the accident several years earlier when a logging truck rammed the car in which Horace's sixteen-year-old daughter was riding, about the expenses related to her hospitalization and death, and about the bank note he paid off on time. With this new knowledge, she pities Horace and for the first time achieves some sense of true grief and of the cause for his obstinate behavior. The next winter, when her furnace quits, her pipes freeze, and her house suffers water damage, she hires Horace to perform the repairs, agreeing to pay his price when he finishes the work. All summer he works on the repairs, and Flora constantly oversees his meticulous, gentle hands at work, even occasionally undergoing "a sensual experience, a feeling very much as if his fingers had touched [her] bare breasts" (12–13). On the day he finally turns on the heat, Horace presents his "bill": "'What I'd like is to accompany you to church next Sunday. Regular service. Hope for you to take my arm going up and down the steps. I want to sit beside you and share a hymnbook. Afterwards be nice for you to introduce me around so I can shake a few hands. . . .

That's my price. . . . You told me you'd pay it. I took your word'" (15). The honest, simple Horace apparently oversteps his station as he seeks his payment. Despite her developing admiration for Horace, Flora experiences genuine shock and then offense at the suggestion that she be seen in the company of an obviously inferior, working man. After all, she is the flower of her town's elite: "Truth is many people looked to me socially because both my father and my Henry had been so prominent in Tobaccoton. I was certainly the best bridge player and the only lady who'd ever been to an inaugural ball at the governor's mansion" (13). Ultimately reprimanded by her pastor, Father Buford, Flora is "laden with guilt" (16) and acquiesces to Horace's request, determined "to hold [her] head high and endure" (17).

On the Sunday, Flora finds herself impressed at Horace's cleanliness and "firm strength" (17). Even Father Buford's sermon on "'The Least of These'" reinforces the irony of Flora and Horace's presence. Despite their different social classes, the two are bound by individual senses of honor and dignity, personal attributes that rise above cultural distinctions. Horace has obviously endured the suffering due to the loss of his daughter, and Flora has survived the deaths of her father and husband, but she has not had to face the traumas of violent death and financial hardship that have shaped Horace's self-respect. Her pity over his situation softens her harshness and allows her to "endure" the certain gossip of her so-called friends, but the developing friendship with Horace yields a fuller, more distinct relationship than any artificially based bond she enjoys with her bridge partners. She abandons the pretenses of her social class and gradually adopts the directness of Horace's class, realizing that truth stings the hearer only for the moment but that truth also destroys the barriers between distinctly different people to produce a stronger bond. She may have inadvertently caused Horace pain because of her upper-class background, but she evolves into a more understanding person that deliberately avoids causing more pain to another by assuming some of that pain. Her highly structured social world is one without chaos, but her involvement with pain allows her to see that world's fallacies more sensibly and to work toward some sort of social justice.

William Hoffman's characters are southerners, most coming from Virginia or the coal regions of West Virginia and southwest Virginia. As southerners, they embody the many traits familiar in southern literary characters: love, honor, pity, pride, compassion, and sacrifice. These are traits fostered by the Old South immediately before and after the American Civil War, but they are also traits that lasted well into the twentieth century and that were idolized by such Southern Renascence writers as Faulkner, Warren, Ransom, and Welty. These writers did not fail to show us the South's underbelly, but they invariably projected the idea that these virtues would overcome the vilest and most ill-mannered supporters of the emerging mechanistic commercialism characterizing the New South.

The South's movement from Old South to New South can be roughly marked by the two World Wars of the twentieth century, with the period between them as the South's early period of transition. Hoffman was born between the two wars, and like many writers born during that period, he shows us a lifestyle in transition, one that may be southern in setting but is universal in values. Tod Young's compromise of values and his eventual failure to live up to the ideals he has established for himself are not surprising, for the world around him has little room for his desired lifestyle. He had been taught obedience and duty and manliness by his father, but Tod's preparation for life has been undermined by his sensitivity and humanity. A century ago, he could have meshed the economic demands with the personal philosophy, but as society becomes increasingly impersonal, it has less tolerance for love, honor, pity, pride, compassion, or sacrifice. These characteristics demand a unique statement through action that is less viable in a society that demands technocratic uniformity.

In *A Walk to the River*, Jackson LeJohn finds a role model in Paul Elgin, who unwillingly sacrifices himself for the common good of his congregation. Jackson's "pain" is, first, his firm belief in the general malevolence of mankind, based largely on his war experiences, and, then, his loss of faith resulting from his wife's death. Wanting to believe that Paul actually attacked Caroline, Jackson abides by his honor to uncover the truth about two people who have repudiated their pasts, and in the process he has his faith restored in mankind, largely, and in God, partially, through the example of one human being unwilling to perform a base act that would destroy the other. Jackson recognizes that Caroline Gaines, like the New South, has sublimated her foundation values in favor of superficial materialism, and Paul Elgin, like the Old South, has found his core values to be largely ineffective in an unstable and uncertain world. Through this paradox, Jackson comes to realize, as does Paul, that revealing the truth as he

knows it will cause more pain and suffering and will ultimately benefit no one: Paul will still lose his pulpit, Caroline will lose her position
and family, and the town will lose its innate innocence. He therefore
opts for the least destructive evil and remains silent about Paul's innocence. Because he must live within his social community, Jackson
favors the concrete here-and-now over an abstract hereafter: "'I don't
know where the truth starts and stops. . . . But if I did, all the truth in
the world isn't as meaningful to me as close flesh and blood'" (283).
As he gives up Paul Elgin for the good of his town, Jackson also re-
news his relationship with his "flesh and blood," Injun, his son.
Affirming his existence in the midst of ever-changing values and suffering, Jackson, at the novel's close, romps with his son in the river,
the very water that is the symbolic source of life and medium of bap-
tism as well as the representation of constant mutability.

Likewise, Peck comprehends the common bond of suffering that
people share in contemporary society. Pity can be as destructive as
gossip to a person's state, and the sharing of pain appeases its sting
for all afflicted, the basis, after all, for Twelve Step self-help programs.
He does not want to confront his own grief, only immerse himself in
it, and he does not readily notice Jenny's grief at her overall condition. Together, though, Peck and Jenny help each other live through
their sorrow and face their daily activities. The result is that the bond
of pain eventually yields a bond of comfort and maybe even joy. But
that ultimate goal can come only when each deliberately avoids inflicting suffering upon the other.

Similarly, Flora finds new strength in an unlikely source with Horace
Puckett as she acknowledges the emotional strength he demonstrates
despite adversities of poverty and death. In a story of manners, void of
violence, Flora realizes that suffering does not stem solely from acute
misfortune and gross improprieties. Often suffering results from simple
ignorance about another's situation or from inadvertent slights. Culture
is based on the precept of one person's superiority over another, and
Flora bases her sense of that superiority on material possessions and
social prominence. As she perceives honor, pride, compassion, and sacrifice in Horace's actions, she gradually gives them more credence in
her own life. Whether she eventually participates in a romantic relationship with Horace is irrelevant, for she develops a respect—a compassion—for him as a human being that overcomes many of the props
that had supported her superior attitude.

In the 1980 interview at Longwood College, William Hoffman said,
"Life shapes and teaches. . . . The purpose for all of us is the shaping

of our lives." In a culture where values are never fixed for long, where personal beliefs are abandoned for societal beliefs, where neither religion nor technology nor commercialism can provide sustaining guidelines, where ten commandments or twelve steps are often too many to remember much less practice, we need a simple guide for our lives. William Hoffman has provided us that basic dictum to help us survive this modern, senseless world: "Cause no one pain."

The Novels of William Hoffman

One Writer's Spiritual Odyssey from World War II

to the Twenty-first Century

William L. Frank

In the forty-five years since William Hoffman published *The Trumpet Unblown,* he has published ten other novels, four collections of short stories, and over fifty uncollected stories. Obviously there are numerous ways to approach a body of fiction this large, written over such a long period of time. In her master's thesis, Mary Davis has suggested that the most striking aspect of Hoffman's novels has to do with the initiation of his male protagonist, and she has skillfully revealed how each novel shows a young man's entry into the real world, either escaping from a sheltered innocence or reentering the world of reality from a position of withdrawal and observation.[1]

Yet if one stands a distance from Hoffman's fictional world and focuses primarily on the novels, he senses that Hoffman's real subject is not initiation, but his own spiritual odyssey. Consequently, I have divided the eleven novels into three groups: (1) the "war novels"— *The Trumpet Unblown* (1955), *Days in the Yellow Leaf* (1958), and *Yancey's War* (1966); these show the effects of war both on the novels' protagonists and on all those with whom he comes in contact following his wartime experiences; (2) the "Virginia/West Virginia novels"— *A Place for My Head* (1960), *The Dark Mountains* (1963), *A Walk to the River* (1970), *A Death of Dreams* (1973), and *Tidewater Blood* (1998); in these novels we discover the importance of place, the fragility of human relationships, the influence of the past upon the present, and the emptiness of material success; and (3) the "philosophical/spiritual novels"—*The Land That Drank the Rain* (1982), *Godfires* (1985), and *Furors Die* (1990); in these, both the central characters and the author struggle with questions of spiritual disillusionment, the possibility of redemption, the enormous power of love to suffocate or bring about renewal, and the apparent failure of religion to provide the means for acceptance or salvation.

Although *The Trumpet Unblown* is actually Hoffman's second novel, it is his first published novel, and we will begin with it. *The*

---

1. Mary H. Davis, "Introduction to the Novels of William Hoffman," master's thesis, Longwood College, Farmville, Va., 1980.

Trumpet Unblown is largely autobiographical, and ironically, because Bill Hoffman in reality is a gentle, caring man, contains more violence and brutality than any of Hoffman's other early novels. A reader quickly discovers the influence of Ernest Hemingway, especially the Hemingway of *A Farewell to Arms* and *For Whom the Bell Tolls,* and the probable influence of Stephen Crane's *The Red Badge of Courage,* especially in scenes and descriptions of military field hospitals where men are depicted as mechanical, detached. But although many of the scenes and characters are based on Hoffman's own experiences in World War II, the novel's protagonist, Tyree Jefferson Shelby, is not William Hoffman. He is a twentieth-century version of Crane's Henry Fleming, becoming in the course of the novel another casualty of the war. Early in the story, Shelby tells Sergeant Moody:

> "I know about the army. I volunteered for it."
> Moody sighed and took a long drink from the bottle.
> "May I ask why."
> "What do you mean why?"
> "Why'd you volunteer?"
> "Because it was right, that's why."
> Moody looked at him a moment, then began to laugh. . . . "I'm sorry," Moody said between the laughter. "I'm sorry but I'd forgotten there were still people who could believe that sort of thing." (59)

But we discover that war does more than change idealism—it destroys it. In a scene near the novel's conclusion, Shelby is back in Richmond, talking with the girl he had left behind, Cannon, who says to him:

> "I was afraid you had fallen in love with some beautiful foreign woman. Did you?"
> "No."
> "You didn't fall in love with anybody?"
> "I fell out of love with a lot of people." (301)

What happens to Shelby between these two scenes is the essence of *The Trumpet Unblown,* and episodes throughout the novel reveal in almost incomprehensible and graphic detail the total inhumanity of man toward his fellow human beings. Whether the horror is that of a violent boxing exhibition between two individuals or that inflicted by one people—the Germans who made up the SS—upon another—the displaced persons of the Nazi-conquered Slavic states—it is unspeakable.

Deadened by the war he had voluntarily entered, Shelby "recovers" in a hospital in Europe, and upon his return to the States is sent to a rehabilitation center, where he puts off as long as he can his eventual return to Richmond. Upon his arrival in Richmond, Shelby realizes that Thomas Wolfe was right—"You can't go home again":

> His furlough was for thirty days, and that was the longest time he ever lived through. He was determined to hurt his parents as little as possible, but hurt was extremely difficult to avoid. His parents' world was such a complex of traditions, honors and loves that there was no language left with which to communicate. (297)

There are no heroes in this novel; only, as Moody has already said, choices between evils, or the lesser of two evils. A case in point is Shelby's choice between Blizzard and Petras. Superficially, there seems no decision on the part of the reader: Blizzard is obviously the worse of the two—cruel, sadistic, unthinking, uncaring, totally devoid of sensitivity, compassion, sentiment, in matters large and small, whether he is defiling a picture of Shelby's girlfriend or literally destroying another human being in a physical encounter. The Greek, Petras, on the other hand, befriends Shelby, at times treats him kindly, even occasionally shares some of his ill-gotten war booty with Shelby; but beneath the skin—under the smiling facade—Petras is every bit as inhuman as Blizzard: he lies, bribes, deceives, treats people with contempt, betrays those who have befriended him, uses German civilians to satisfy his physical needs, and in the final brutal and bloody encounter with Blizzard, inflicts unnecessary humiliation and pain upon the already beaten Blizzard.

The book's title announces that there will be no heroes in this saga of World War II, that the trumpet will not only not blow for Tyree Shelby, it will not blow for any of the assorted characters of death and destruction in this novel. Such a rich and complex book has many primary and secondary themes, but ultimately this book reflects a belief that despite everything encountered, there will be a tomorrow for humanity, and perhaps—we can at least hope so—that tomorrow will be bright. At one point late in the novel, Shelby's closest friend, Sergeant Moody, who has witnessed all that Shelby has seen, expresses a basic optimism that denies at least some of the lingering horror created by many of the novel's scenes:

> "You know," Moody said one day when he and Shelby were lying in the sun, "sometimes I get a crazy thought."
> "What's that?"
> "I think maybe the human race will survive in spite of everything."
> "The sun feels good all right."
> "That's what I mean. Maybe there's hope for a man who can enjoy the sun." (197)

Although *Days in the Yellow Leaf* was the first novel Hoffman wrote, it was not published until after *The Trumpet Unblown*. *Days in the Yellow Leaf* remains Hoffman's favorite among his current production of eleven novels,[2] possibly simply because it was his first. More likely, however, he recalls it with special affection because it contains almost all of the motifs and themes, directly or indirectly, that dominate his work. First, there is the son's search for his relationship with a distant father, which also appears in *A Place for My Head, Godfires,* and *Furors Die*. Second, there is the mindless brutality that occurs in a cold and seemingly meaningless world. We have already witnessed this theme in *The Trumpet Unblown,* and we see it again and again in his other works. In *Days in the Yellow Leaf,* for example, the novel's protagonist, Tod Young, is held by an accomplice while the novel's bully, Pinky Lemon, administers a mind-deadening beating with a wrapped bicycle chain. Third, there are the devastating and endless effects of war, a theme of course prevalent in Hoffman's three war novels. Fourth, there is the theme of a world ruled ruthlessly by the rich and powerful, which we see again in *A Walk to the River, The Dark Mountains, A Death of Dreams, Godfires,* and *Furors Die*. And a final motif involves the protagonist's attempts to understand himself, the world, which he has not created, and those whom he loves so deeply.

Hoffman's second published novel takes its title from Byron's "On This Day I Complete My Thirty-sixth Year": "My days are in the yellow leaf; / The flowers and fruits of love are gone"; from the novel's open-

2. William Hoffman, conversation with the author, July 22, 1990, Charlotte Court House, Va.

ing scenes until its close, the reader feels that he is witnessing the inevitable playing out of a classic Greek tragedy. Tod Young's main problems center around his inability to accept his father, the epitome of the self-made business man: a former junk dealer who has clawed his way to the top during the Great Depression, he is now president of one of the two local banks—a strong man, a fighter, a hunter. Tod, on the other hand, is sensitive, compassionate, and in his father's eyes too tender, not tough enough for the world in which Tod must live. The novel, divided into six parts, opens with a brief history of Tod's father (symbolically named Will), Tod, and the novel's other principal characters, that tells us how these characters happened to find themselves, in the year following World War II, together in a small town "over the mountains from Virginia." We quickly discover that before Tod is thirty he has been a conscientious objector (over the strong objections of his father, who labels him a coward and a quitter), a highly decorated hero of World War II, a preministerial student, a newspaper reporter, and finally a loan officer in his father's bank. Along the way, Tod had thought "and believed he had discovered the principle he was looking for. He decided about the only thing a man could do was to live without hurting. . . . He made himself a promise he would never hurt anyone again" (106).

But the lesson that Tod learns in the course of the novel is that we hurt without intending, that despite all the care we take to avoid it, we hurt most keenly those who are closest to us. Tod spends half of his free time protecting Danny Little, "a little man with a bald head and a limp," who had shot his own kneecap off during the war to get out of combat and who ended up serving time in Leavenworth. There, he slowly lost his nerve, his dignity, and his mind; upon his release from prison, he is one of the town's derelicts, teased, bruised, and belittled by the bullies who inhabit all of Hoffman's worlds. When Danny is forced to play pool for money and loses badly, and Tod is unable to help because his father refuses his request for an advance on his salary, Danny cashes a bad check; following his arrest, he hangs himself in his cell to avoid going back to jail for an extended sentence. Tod, unable to forgive his father for refusing to help, seeks escape in his marriage to Grace.

Initially, the marriage is a good one; the couple appear genuinely in love. But Tod refuses to remain in the house his father had given them as a wedding present, and when Grace falls while trying to hang curtains in their small apartment, and the baby they are expecting is delivered stillborn, the relationship disintegrates. Grace sleeps with

Tod's best friend, and Tod, in a scene reminiscent of Greek tragedy, slays the two lovers with a pair of shotgun blasts. The seeming inevitability of the evolving action recalls Robert Penn Warren's image of the spiderweb in the Cass Mastern episode of *All the King's Men:*

> Cass Mastern lived for a few years and in that time he learned that the world is all of one piece. He learned that the world is like an enormous spider web and if you touch it, however lightly, at any point, the vibration ripples to the remotest perimeter and the drowsy spider feels the tingle and is drowsy no more but springs out to fling the gossamer coils about you who have touched the web and then inject the black, numbing poison under your hide. It does not matter whether or not you meant to brush the web of things. Your happy foot or your gay wing may have brushed it ever so lightly, but what happens always happens and there is the spider, bearded black and with his great faceted eyes glittering like mirrors in the sun, or like God's eye, and the fangs dripping.[3]

The only relief to this otherwise increasingly darkening tale is the reconciliation between Will and Tod that takes place in part 6, a single chapter of only seven pages, almost an epilogue. It occurs as Will walks into his library as Tod is in the act of taking a .30-06 Husquarna from his father's gun cabinet, intending to commit suicide:

> "No," he said, coming to Tod and taking the rifle out of his hand. He ejected the shell, leaned back against the wall, and clasped the rifle to himself. "No," he said, putting his face in his hand and shaking it.
> "Forgive me," Tod said, taking hold of his arm. "Please forgive me."
> Suddenly they were holding each other tightly, the rifle pressed between them. Tod led him to a chair and knelt beside it. . . .
> "I won't do it again," Tod said, taking hold of the hand. "I promise." . . .
> "Forgive me," Tod said.
> His father held him close.
> "A father doesn't have to forgive his son anything."
> They stood together, still holding each other. (352–53)

Although *Yancey's War* was not the next of Hoffman's published works, it clearly belongs to the "war novels" group. As the novel's

---

3. Robert Penn Warren, *All the King's Men* (New York: Harcourt, Brace and Co., 1946), 200.

dust jacket reveals, it is a novel "about two unsuitable soldiers, one man's wife, and the wartime army." *Yancey's War* is the first of several of Hoffman's novels to employ the device of a dual protagonist, and the title itself conveys the concept of a dual reference; first, that World War II becomes for Marvin Yancey "his war." But more importantly, the title also suggests the internal conflict, or war, within Yancey as he tries to come to terms with the fact that the medals awarded him during the First World War not only were unearned but ironically were given him because he was the sole survivor of his platoon—a survivor only because he deserted his comrades when the shooting began.

At the novel's opening the point of view is that of a first-person narrator, initially focusing on Yancey: "Unlike the rest of us, Marvin Yancey was not young" (1). Yancey obviously is both out of shape and out of place with the younger inductees:

> . . . At twenty-five I was near the average age. A few were in their early and middle thirties. Yancey, however, was well into his forties.
> He sagged in the yellow-hot sun like a stick of butter set on end.
> The soft blubber of his rolypoly body hung over his shirt collar and drooped about his belt. The web belt itself seemed to be keeping his belly from popping out of his shirt and spilling to the ground. As he stood at attention, he made me think of a slapstick comedian who at any instant would go into an act ridiculing the Army. (2)

The reader soon discovers that unlike most older men in the unit, Yancey is a volunteer, not a draftee. He soon attaches himself to the novel's other protagonist, Charles Elgar, despite Elgar's wish that Yancey would leave him alone:

> I couldn't escape him. He followed me into latrines and squeezed beside me at the mess hall. In ranks he maneuvered to stand next to me. He pretended not to see my annoyance. Wherever I looked, I met his watery, winking eyes. (5)

Elgar shortly discovers a second odd fact about Marvin Yancey; in addition to being a volunteer, he reveals during routine questioning for future assignment that he is a veteran of World War I, having served in the infantry in France. But Elgar and the other men of the unit learn something else about Yancey during basic training, and that is that Marvin Yancey is an unprincipled brownnoser, briber, and con artist, who gets out of KP by buttering up the cooks and apple-polishing the noncoms: "On Monday everybody except Yancey was again assigned to KP" (19).

Yancey soon discovers that not everyone in the army can be conned. Their basic training platoon sergeant, "a hulking Slav named Bulgan," recognizes Yancey for what he is and is determined to run Yancey out of the army (28). He gives him "double time around the drill field," extra marching drills and exercises, and zeros in on using the obstacle course as Yancey's Waterloo (32). But Yancey's medals save him where his conniving, conning, and brownnosing could not.

As the unit nears the end of basic training, Yancey confides to Elgar, who has been planning all along to apply to OCS, that he, too, intends to apply, and Elgar, having seen how Yancey could talk or con his way through basic, begins to wonder if Yancey could help him get into and through OCS. Thus the stage is set for the two to attend OCS together. But before OCS there is a seven-day furlough, and after visiting his family in Richmond, Virginia, for a few days, Elgar accepts Yancey's invitation to visit him at his home outside of Washington, D.C. There begins an initiation for Charles Elgar that is to affect him profoundly for the rest of the novel, for on his first night at Yancey's home, Yancey's wife, Martha, offers herself to him:

> "There's nothing to be afraid of," she told me, her voice completely calm. She could have been discussing a flower arrangement. "We share separate rooms, and he won't come looking for me. He's drunk."
>
> She leaned to the night table to use the ashtray. At the same moment she smiled—a smile no longer thin and cold. Rather it was lascivious. On her proper, ladylike face it was shocking.
>
> With a slow, deliberate movement, she crushed out the cigarette, stood, and crossed to my bed. Her housecoat rustled. I smelled her perfume. She sat beside me, and the bed sank under her weight.
>
> "It's chilly out here," she said, hugging herself. "Why don't you let me in there with you." (79)

Although Elgar, afraid of a sudden appearance by Yancey, refuses Martha's advances on this occasion, the stage is set for a later and more lasting relationship. When Charles and Yancey return from their leaves, they both enter OCS. Yancey manages to bribe his way through, but Elgar piles up enough demerits for minor infractions, many of which were caused by Yancey, that he flunks out. Sent to a new camp where a new unit is being formed, Elgar—partially to get even with Yancey—calls Martha and invites her to visit him. Much to his surprise she accepts, and Martha and he begin an idyllic interlude during which he falls in love with Martha.

Elgar soon discovers, however, that he is but one in a chain of Martha's conquests. He visits Martha while on furlough when Yancey is away, and she informs him that she is in love with another man. Hurt and bewildered, feeling more like a lost little boy than a jilted lover, Charles leaves that same evening, returns to his home in Richmond in a daze, and then almost immediately to his army base, feeling "old, tired, and without hope" (226).

When Elgar's battalion is finally sent overseas even though the war is already winding down, he suffers the cruel irony of discovering that his number one personal enemy, Yancey, now a captain, is his immediate commanding officer. Yancey, however, is so totally inept as a leader that his superior officers transfer a majority of his enlisted men into other units as replacements, and Yancey is given command of a single line laundry unit, and sent to serve the then-advancing and soon victorious American army. But ironically the allied military successes have stretched the supply lines too thin, and Yancey's company is alerted for a move into Germany. Yancey, however, still has not learned how to read a military map, and as the hours tick by without their making contact with the American forces, Elgar and the other men in the unit realize that Yancey is lost and has led them into a literal no-man's-land.

As the convoy of laundry trucks, led by Yancey in his jeep, snakes its way through the narrow streets of an unnamed town, one of the men whispers to Elgar that he thinks he has seen a German soldier at a window. Within a few minutes the road is blocked by a German personnel carrier, and simultaneously windows open, German soldiers appear, and burp guns erupt in a steady stream of bullets. The company is split, and Elgar, Yancey, and five others seek refuge in a house that will become for many a tomb. For two days and nights the rapidly diminishing band hold off German flamethrowers, grenade attacks, and an almost constant stream of small-arms fire, but on the third day the rumbling approach of a German tank all but guarantees their collective deaths. It is at this point in the novel that Yancey becomes an unwilling hero. Knowing full well that his cowardly actions during the siege will disgrace him for eternity, Yancey takes a home-made gasoline bomb, crawls out on the roof of the house, and lobs the bomb in the direction of the tank, stopping it in its tracks. Several hours later, hearing nothing in the street and receiving no German fire, Charles ventures forth waving a white flag, but there are no Germans left to accept his surrender. Later Elgar asks, almost rhetorically, how Yancey could have done it: How could the most cowardly of all, facing certain death, have willingly given up his life to take out the German tank? It is the soldier nicknamed the Professor who replies:

> "Human beings now and then are capable of rising above themselves. Only now and then, but it's the best part of us. No matter how corrupt, degraded, and filthy we become, we can commit acts which are far more than the total of ourselves. If I've learned anything, it's that a man brave for one second—and everybody has a second of bravery in him—can change the course of history." (368)

In Yancey's final and heroic action, there is a lesson for the young Charles Elgar, and indeed for all of us.

The second group of Hoffman's novels, the five Virginia/West Virginia novels, are set in rural areas or small towns of the region and are concerned as much with the influence of the past upon the present as they are with the present. These works reveal Hoffman's knowledge and understanding of the land and its people as the characters strive, frequently without success, to pursue relationships and self-understanding that will enable them to achieve goals if not to realize dreams.

The fictional setting of Hoffman's third published novel, *A Place for My Head,* has a real counterpart; the town of McCloud is based on Farmville, Virginia, and the novel's King County is a thinly disguised Prince Edward County. The story revolves around Angus McCloud, a young but spiritually dead lawyer. A descendent of the once prominent family for whom the town was named, he has not too skillfully presided over the selling of his patrimony; the family's original four thousand acres is presently reduced to two hundred. (In certain ways the disintegration of the McCloud family brings to mind the decline of the Compsons, so vividly captured in William Faulkner's *The Sound and the Fury,* although Angus McCloud is a much more sympathetic character than is Jason Compson.) Hoffman suggests the sterility both of the land and of Angus in an early scene when Angus's perpetual date, Laura Lee, chides him for his excessive drinking:

> "I'm not drunk. I wish I were. God I wish I were."
> "Well, it's not nice. That's why my father doesn't like you."
> Angus started to answer, then shut his mouth and drove on. She was dead. They were both dead. They belonged in the cemetery. Even then there would be nothing to write on the tombstones, no dates of birth, no lines of endearment, nothing but two slabs of blank marble shining in the moonlight. (52)

The totality of Angus's despair is deftly revealed in a scene in which he attempts to engage Laura Lee in a sexual encounter:

> "I'm sorry, Angus. It would just be silly."
> "You could have tried. It wouldn't have hurt either of us. It might have conceivably helped one of us." . . .
> "It's too late for us. Maybe we've known each other for too long."
> He started the car. He had known all along it would come to this. They were both dead, and had he succeeded, that too would have been dead—an obscene, mechanical act. (64)

Angus's potential salvation and redemption appear temporarily in the person of Mrs. Caroline Gainer, a woman Angus has worshiped since boyhood. Following a chance meeting, Caroline encourages a romantic interest between herself and Angus, but Angus fails to realize that Caroline is leading him on only in the hope of making her husband, George, jealous. Angus, believing he has a chance to claim Caroline for his own, builds up his law practice by winning a suit for a black client against one of the leading families of McCloud. Believing a false rumor of a new international corporation's moving its headquarters to Southside, he also foolishly and hastily enters into a partnership to develop most of the remaining family estate by building houses on speculation. He even voluntarily seeks help for his growing dependence on alcohol at an alcoholic treatment center in nearby Richmond—all for the sake of wooing Caroline and winning her from her husband.

Angus's world crumbles when first George and then Caroline let him know that they are back together, stronger in their love and relationship than before:

"I love him," Caroline said, raising her face. "I can't help that, can I? You can't help who you love. I did my best. I can't help it if I couldn't love you." (395)

He was able to keep going for a while. His life had a certain momentum which pushed him on whether he cared or not. . . . Even the great loneliness didn't kill. After a while the pain dulled somewhat, and he entered a kind of twilight zone in which there were no emotions. (400)

Angus slept a good deal. He fixed his own meals, opening a package of soda crackers and a ten-cent tin of Vienna sausage. He wandered through the house at night. And he sat in the chair staring out the window—rocking, rocking, rocking. (406)

A Place for My Head calls to mind two earlier classic American novels. One can compare it to F. Scott Fitzgerald's *The Great Gatsby,* in that Angus's dream is similar to that of Jay Gatsby in his pursuit of Daisy, and in both novels the destruction of the dream is equally disastrous. Daisy Buchanan in many of her actions is certainly like Hoffman's Caroline Gainer, and when both characters decide to return to their respective husbands, the worlds of Jay Gatsby and Angus McCloud cave in. Similarly, *A Place for My Head* can be compared to Theodore Dreiser's *Sister Carrie:* Both novels end with their protagonists' dreams interrupted if not wholly dashed, and both novels end with their protagonists looking out a window and "rocking, rocking, rocking"—an action that suggests motion without direction or advancement, similar to the imagery in T. S. Eliot's "Prufrock," such as the "pair of ragged claws" that move about at the bottom of the ocean.

My discussion of Hoffman's fourth novel, *The Dark Mountains,* is abbreviated here, since it is brilliantly discussed by Martha E. Cook in her contribution to the present collection. It is impossible to suggest in a few pages the range, scope, and depth of Hoffman's study of the coal industry in this novel, or to do justice to some of the finest character studies in modern American literature. As W. L. Frank Jr. has suggested earlier:

It is difficult to determine just who the protagonist is in the novel. Is it James MacGlauglin, the owner of the mines worth millions of dollars, who rose from nothing? Is it James (Jamie) St. George, James's grandson, who loves his mother's father, James, but despises his own father, a do-nothing alcoholic and trans-

planted Virginia aristocrat? Or is it Paul Crittenden, the college
friend of Jamie's who leaves his once wealthy but now financially
troubled family in the comforts of Richmond, Virginia, to enter
the West Virginia wilderness and work in James's coal mines?[4]

When William Hoffman discusses *The Dark Mountains,* he invokes
Robert Penn Warren's *All the King's Men,* which Hoffman calls "a most
beautifully crafted book." Following one of Warren's techniques in that
novel, Hoffman uses the dual protagonist, as Mary Davis has argued.[5]
Also, just as Warren used Huey Long to characterize Willie Stark,
Hoffman bases the character of James MacGlauglin on Hoffman's own
great-grandfather, an uneducated Scottish immigrant. Hoffman's fasci-
nation with coal mining led him to talk at length with miners as well as
to visit operating coal mines as he gathered materials for this novel.
The result is a highly realistic novel that traces three generations of the
coal-mining MacGlauglin family during the years of the development of
labor unions. It is James MacGlauglin who accomplishes the American
dream. He builds his own town, an industry, and a dynasty from the
rich coal veins of the mountains of West Virginia, and he lives long
enough to see the decline and fall of his kingdom, first assaulted and
weakened by the miners' union and finally occupied by U.S. Army
troops.

Not only does James rule his miners with an iron hand, but he
rules his family in much the same fashion. His family has problems:
his daughter and only surviving child, Sara, is busy with her own children, who are her crosses to bear; his grandson, Jamie, is a woman-
izer and will do anything to keep from being like his weak and
pseudoaristocratic father, William St. George; and Faith, his grand-
daughter, is a delicate, sickly young woman who tries to protect her
father from the roughness of the MacGlauglins. Into the midst of this
family, invited by Jamie, comes Paul Crittenden. He learns much—
good and bad—from his association with the MacGlauglins.

Although the novel's major conflict exists between James and the
labor unions, it is Paul Crittenden who gradually moves to center
stage. James, believing that his land is God-given, that he is being "re-
warded for taking risks and undergoing hardships," (359) tries des-

4. William L. Frank Jr., "William Hoffman's *The Dark Mountains,*" unpublished
paper, 1983.
5. Hoffman, conversation with author; Davis, "Introduction to the Novels."

perately to keep the unions out of his mountains and out of his coal-fields. He has worked long and hard to build up his empire and cannot see any justice in the union's efforts. But it is Paul, looking to the future, who ultimately brings order, maturity, and stability to the family. In this respect Paul resembles both Jack Burden of *All the King's Men* and Nick Carraway of *The Great Gatsby* in that, by novel's end, he is ready to take his justly earned place in the world he has helped to mold and create. Thus, *The Dark Mountains* is, as Mary Davis has demonstrated, both an initiation novel and a novel about "the resiliency of the human spirit."

Hoffman's sixth novel, *A Walk to the River,* is told by a first-person narrator, Jackson LeJohn, a broken, dispirited man of only forty-two. Hoffman's opening sentence describes Jackson as "a dead man who sat . . ." (11); his first description of another important character in the novel, Doc Setter, intensifies the mood and tone: "I'd never seen Setter when he didn't appear tired. . . . Like me, he was a mournful man. . . . He knew mortality and death the way some men knew their wives, and it'd killed the spirit in him" (12).

But Jackson is shocked into reality by Doc Setter's explanation of the reason for his early morning visit: "A member of the congregation claims his wife was lechered" (13). Not only is the accuser the most important man in town, Lou Gaines, aggressive, wealthy, influential, but the man he accuses in the small town of Black Leaf is the church's minister, Reverend Paul Elgin, and because Jackson is the reluctant chairman of the church's board it is his lot to carry out the investigation—to separate fact from rumor and speculation. While Jackson is shocked by Setter's story, when left alone, he describes himself as "a man holding a rattlesnake: no way to let go without being bit" (16). In this way, Hoffman sets up the principal thrust of the story: Jackson LeJohn's pursuit of the truth behind Preacher Paul Elgin's alleged sexual assault on Caroline Gaines, the beautiful, haughty, aristocratic wife of Black Leaf's leading citizen.

Jackson soon discovers more truth than he had wished for, for not only had Elgin led a wild and turbulent life before his ordination, but so, too, had Caroline Gaines, before her marriage to Lou. Counting on Jackson's confidence and integrity, Caroline confirms what Jackson has learned: She and Paul had known each other extremely well "in another country." Caroline, however, has no intention of losing what she has fought so hard to acquire; she will neither pressure her husband to withdraw the charges, nor admit before an open hearing with the congregation to her earlier life with Paul.

On the day appointed for the hearing—a hot, sweltering, summer day—the church is packed, newspaper reporters are everywhere, and Jackson must preside over the congregational meeting of the pastor and his parishioners. Once the formality of reading minutes is accomplished, Jackson announces that "The floor's open," and immediately Lou Gaines stands: "I'm charging the minister of this church with assaulting my wife. I'm charging him with invading my home and attempting rape" (303). In the brief debate that follows it is evident to all that Paul will lose. Every time he scores a point with the church members, Lou Gaines rises to remind them of what Paul did to his wife.

The vote against Paul is overwhelming, although not unanimous, and the next day a sadder but perhaps not much wiser Jackson LeJohn goes to the manse, wishes Paul well, and watches as Paul, his wife, Helen, and their children drive out of town in a battered, dirty, smoke-belching old Dodge. The novel ends with Jackson and his son at the river, Jackson determined to see to it that his long-neglected son at least "got all his boyhood," and realizing that perhaps he, Jackson, wasn't dead after all: "I bit down on my sadness. I thought that even pain had goodness. A dead man couldn't suffer. To grieve, a man had to be alive and to care about something" (336).

One could argue that the novel's principal theme is one of stoical acceptance. But at the same time, while the evidence is not yet complete on the influence of Hemingway on Hoffman, certainly Jackson's struggles throughout the novel remind the reader of the principal characteristics of Hemingway's code hero. Whether the comparison be to Santiago of *The Old Man and the Sea,* Robert Wilson of "The Short Happy Life of Frances Macomber," or Pedro Romero of *The Sun Also Rises,* Jackson's actions display many of the characteristics of the code hero—persistence, daring, playing by the rules of the game, adherence to what is right, discharging one's responsibilities, accepting the consequences of one's own actions, fair-mindedness. Jackson adheres to all of these as he seeks the truth about Paul Elgin and Caroline Gaines, traveling the different paths that each took to Black Leaf, Virginia, and the night of their "walk to the river."

Hoffman's seventh novel, and the fourth of what I have called his Virginia/West Virginia novels, is masterfully analyzed by Dabney

Stuart later in this collection. Indeed, to say anything about it here would appear redundant. Suffice it to say that *A Death of Dreams* is another story of a spiritual odyssey, this time about Guy Dion, who although not completely spiritually dead, is slowly dying, reminiscent of many of Graham Greene's characters in such novels as *A Burnt-Out Case* and *The Heart of the Matter.* Guy, an enormously successful businessman but a less-successful husband and father, agrees upon his wife's urging to enter Westfield, a hospital close to Richmond, Virginia, for a brief period of rest and recovery from his "nerves." Almost immediately Guy realizes that he is in a hospital for the treatment of alcoholics and other deserters and refugees from the twentieth century's success-oriented and -dominated society. When he meets with the chief physician of the hospital to seek a release because he feels he does not belong there, Guy discovers to his horror that he has been betrayed by his wife and two children—that he has been legally committed.

While a major portion of the novel centers around Guy's hospital treatment and his discovery of many former friends and business associates among the patients, the novel's high point occurs after he engineers his escape. He flees to the mountains where he had grown up (for Hoffman, mountains are almost always symbols of power, serenity, strength, and hope for the future). Hoffman leaves Guy in the mountains, like those in Eliot's *Waste Land,* thinking of "ways to put his house in order" (324).

Hoffman's most recent novel, *Tidewater Blood,* and the last of what I have termed his Virginia/West Virginia novels, belongs in this category rather than the philosophical/spiritual group primarily because of its setting, plot, and themes. The setting shifts between Tidewater Virginia and the now-deserted coalfields of the mountains of West Virginia. The story involves the return of the novel's protagonist, Charlie LeBlanc, to West Virginia to learn about his family's past. This investigation of the protagonist's past most clearly distinguishes *Tidewater Blood* from Hoffman's other novels of the eighties and nineties. Just as the Cass Mastern episode of *All the King's Men* is essential to Jack Burden's acceptance of the past in that novel, so too is Charlie's quest for the secrets of his own father's beginnings in West Virginia before Charlie can again live in the present.

Tidewater Blood begins with a brief prologue in which we learn that a powerful Tidewater Virginia aristocratic family, while gathered to celebrate its 250-year founding, is blown to pieces while standing on the portico of the family mansion. The attention of the investigating authorities is immediately and solely focused on the black sheep of the family, Charles MacKay LeBlanc. Charlie, a Vietnam vet, has brought shame and humiliation to the proud LeBlanc family because he had been court-martialed, sent to Leavenworth, and given a dishonorable discharge. He in turn has repudiated the LeBlanc name, taking the name Jim Moultrie, a name he says he took from a tombstone in Tampa, Florida.

But there are too many people in Tidewater and King County who remember Charlie, what he looks like, and what he had done to earn the animosity of his own family, so it is *Charlie LeBlanc* that the reader follows throughout the novel.

When Charlie is apprehended by the authorities he is staying in a shack at Lizard Inlet on the Chesapeake Bay, existing on vegetables grown in his garden and oysters and fish from the salty marshes. Taken in handcuffs to the county seat, Jessup's Wharf, Charlie is viciously maltreated by the sheriff's deputies, who assume his guilt. Because there is no solid evidence against Charlie he is released with the provision that he sign in at the local jail each morning by eight, and he is forbidden to leave the county. But Charlie knows that unless he proves his innocence he will indeed be found guilty, and given the multiple murders, he will in all probability be sentenced to death for the crime.

What relates this novel to the earlier novels of the Virginia/West Virginia category is Charlie's discovery of the sources of his family's wealth and the influence of previous generations of the LeBlanc family upon the members of the present generation. *Tidewater Blood* has essentially two main threads running through it. First, it is a story of self-discovery and self-realization on Charlie's part; one of Hoffman's major achievements in the course of the novel is the deftness and skill with which he transforms Charles LeBlanc from his initial appearance as a dirty, smelly hermit to a human being with daring, courage, ingenuity, and integrity, an evolution that grows on the reader along with the novel. But, at the same time, *Tidewater Blood* is also a novel of revenge. Who could have hated all living descendants of the LeBlanc family passionately enough to arrange for their simultaneous deaths? And who had the ingenuity to plan and carry out the wholesale murders without placing himself in jeopardy, while at the same time see to it that the authorities and everyone else even remotely connected with the LeBlanc name would assume that the murderer was Charles MacKay LeBlanc? The murderer had intended to place the sole survivor of the LeBlanc name in the custody of the state, which would surely execute him for the multiple murders—thus obliterating the LeBlanc name from the face of the earth.

Through a process worthy of Poe's detective, C. Auguste Dupin, Charlie soon reaches the conclusion that the solution to the crime lies not at the LeBlanc mansion in King County, but in the coalfields of West Virginia, the source of the LeBlanc wealth. Branded as a known felon and fugitive, Charlie heads for the hills and mountains of West Virginia, hounded by state police from two states, and narrowly escaping arrest on several occasions. Along the way he is aided by a wonderful cast of characters, the majority of them also outcasts and dropouts from society: Arthur Moss, a retired salesman and amateur historian; Blackie, a young, tough widow trying to make a living running a bar and truck stop; Cornstalk Skagg, a friend of man who literally lives in a cave; Aunt Jessie, an elderly mountain woman; Zeke Webb, an old army buddy from his days in Vietnam; and Dr. Alexander B. Bingham, a community college physics teacher. Befriended by the friendless, Charlie begins to unlock terrible secrets from the LeBlanc past.

How Hoffman puts all of these ingredients together and solves the riddles behind the multiple murders is, of course, the essence of *Tidewater Blood*. But in writing this novel, William Hoffman is not merely writing a mystery novel, or an interesting and entertaining classic "whodunit." Hoffman is still very much the master of language, point of view, setting, characterization, and scene. With a single sentence Hoffman can evoke the isolation and loneliness of his fugitive protagonist: "People flowed around me as if I were a rock in a stream, especially the alarmed ladies" (45). Or consider Charlie's state of mind during one of his visits to Bellerive, the LeBlanc family estate: "Drinking from the bottle I allowed no childhood memories to take full shape. When they attempted to emerge, I dismembered them" (76).

It is Hoffman's insistence that no one can master the present without understanding and accepting the past that clearly places *Tidewater Blood* in the Virginia/West Virginia phase of his work.

Of the eleven novels under consideration in this essay, three have clearly been labeled Hoffman's war novels and five treated together

as his Virginia/West Virginia novels; yet the next three to be discussed are also set in roughly the same geographical region. Why,
then, the separate treatment? The answer to that question will be
better explained as we discuss these three novels, but one reason for
the grouping is suggested by the dates of publication for all of the
novels: the first seven novels were published between 1955 and 1973,
with intervals of no more than four years between any two, and with
several published within two years of their predecessors. Yet the last
of the first seven novels was published in 1973, and the first of the
last four in 1982, a span of nine years. It is my suggestion that what
ties these three novels together and at the same time clearly separates them from his earlier work is Hoffman's growing concern with
the question of morality and—because the two are intertwined in the
minds of many twentieth-century readers—the role that religion
plays or fails to play in our daily lives. Thus, I describe these three
novels as his philosophical/spiritual novels, and I suggest that the
nine-year interval between *A Death of Dreams* and *The Land That
Drank the Rain* was for William Hoffman a period of contemplation,
deliberation, and resolution.

Although other critics have noted the similarity between *The Land
That Drank the Rain* and Thoreau's *Walden,* I believe that the most
compelling aspects of Hoffman's book are the profusion of religious
symbols and biblical allusions and the Christian themes of innocence, awareness, recognition, and redemption.

The novel focuses initially on the attempt of its symbolically
named protagonist, Claytor Carson, to rid himself of the sin, degrada-
tion, and shame that had come to characterize his materialist life in
California. In an obviously symbolic journey to the East, Clay seeks
salvation in an abandoned coalfield in the mountains of Kentucky,
where, in contact and conflict with a stream of minor characters, Clay
undergoes the modern equivalent of the trials of Job. The novel
opens with Clay's attempts to dissociate himself completely from his
past. He is in the process of burning his nearly new Cadillac Eldorado
and burying it at an illegal dump:

> Hillbillies had slowed their Fords and Chevys . . . to sling refuse
> into the dismal riverbed. Skeletons of cars were down there—
> rusty, weed-twined, toppled into the dark, shallow water. . . .
> Claytor stepped away from the Caddy. It drifted forward . . . he
> struck the barn match and threw it through the rear window. . . .

> An explosion shoved him backwards as fire singed his face.... The Caddy settled on a side like an animal lying down.... Seats boiled and split like flesh.... Earth around the pyre became moist and steamed.... For a time he scented the Caddy's corpse. (1, 2)

For the next several days Clay's life becomes a process of purgation. He builds a small pile of the Caddy's registration papers; his driver's license; his credit, insurance, and country club membership cards; and business cards from "men he's lunched and plotted with: bankers, engineers, lawyers.... He built a tepee of everything and struck a barn match." Later, we are told, he is still seen "casting things off. He owned a wristwatch that ran silently, a battery from another life pushing time through the mechanism.... He climbed to a rise" and "threw it as far as he could" (10, 11).

Determined to wrest a living from the land, Clay "worried that the land was so wounded nothing would grow" (9). But with the arrival of spring his hopes for a new start quicken.

> He looked at the sun, and it appeared larger and a brighter yellow.... He felt warmth settling around him....
> He heard water everywhere. Wrinkles of the land filled. Streams that had never appeared on the land before flowed in pale gullies. His waterfall was so thickened it surged far beyond the stone basin and splashed on rocks well down the channel. (17–18)

Thus far the images have been suggestive and evocative, rather than direct. One recalls Fitzgerald's descriptions of the wasteland on Gatsby's Long Island, or those of T. S. Eliot throughout much of his *Waste Land*. Surely the pyres that destroy the symbols of Clay's materialistic life suggest Eliot's purgatorial and cleansing fires of Buddha's "Fire Sermon" and Augustine's "Lord, Thou pluckst me burning." But Hoffman's Claytor is still a long way from recovery and redemption, and it is here, early in the novel, that the reader meets one of the most unlikely means to grace and salvation in any fictional world. If ever an author has created a character with whom the reader undergoes a constantly changing love-hate relationship, that character is Hoffman's Vestil Skank, the illegitimate son of Renna Skank and any one of twenty-eight members of a high school football team.

Vestil passes himself off to Clay as Nash Shawnee, a song-writing, guitar-playing, would-be entertainer, in the hope of convincing Clay to finance his career and launch his professional debut. He watches Clay constantly, hoping to discover some secret about Clay's background that would give him a hold over Clay. When Clay, not wishing to have any relationship with anyone, repeatedly runs Vestil off and reports Vestil's illegal moonshine still to the local sheriff, Vestil seeks vengeance by assuming the role of Job's tormentor. He sets fire to Clay's cabin, uproots his garden vegetables, and at night sledgehammers down the newly mortared stones that Clay has set by day.

Vestil has been repudiated by his own family—his mother had long ago deserted him and his father could never acknowledge him. Even Vestil's own grandfather labels him "'A child of sin. . . . The print of Satan's on his back, a birthmark like a brown moon. . . . I tried to keep it off him. . . . I believed I could sear evil from him with the hot power of Jehovah's word, but he smelled out sin like a stallion sniffing mares'" (86). And yet Vestil's cries to escape from the mountains before they overwhelm him become prayers that Claytor ultimately responds to: "'Oh, God, I got to get out. Jesus, ain't anybody listening? I got to go'" (61). Vestil "began crying. He was a kernel of sick young flesh swaying and weeping by the lifeless river" (109). He "looked so small and vulnerable on the river bank, folded, an embryo on its feet, his skinny arms helpless white lines. Why, Claytor thought, he's a child" (108). It is this view of Vestil that prompts Clay to regard him in a totally different light and to determine to help him escape his seeming fate. The view of Vestil that Claytor has at this moment is sudden, unexpected, and almost visionary.

But Clay's desire to help Vestil is interrupted by the sudden and wholly unexpected appearance of Clay's wife, Bea, and her malicious attempt to entice him once again into their former, perverse ways. Throughout the novel, from flashbacks and in bits and pieces, the reader has been putting together Clay's story, and the events and incidents that have driven him eastward to seek expiation, redemption, and ultimately, resurrection.

If Bea had accompanied Clay to his own personal hell, and if Vestil becomes the means to Clay's eventual salvation, it is William Hoffman himself who insists on the biblical parallels one finds in this novel. Early in the novel, during Clay's first contacts with Vestil, Vestil throws a stone at Clay as he works in his garden:

> Claytor tried to dodge, but it struck his hip and caused him to stumble.

> "I hope I broke a bone!" Vestil shouted. "You got any idea how
> hard I had to work to get money for that stuff? I hope your blood
> runs on the ground and the damn dogs lick it!" (88)

In one stunning line Hoffman recalls the biblical story of King Ahab
who had done "evil in the sight of the Lord," and to whom the Lord
said, "In the place where dogs licked the blood of Naboth shall dogs
lick thy blood, even then . . . because thou has sold thyself to work
evil in the sight of the Lord."[6]

There is another character in *The Land That Drank the Rain* who, although seemingly minor, plays a significant role in Clay's eventual redemption. Although no single prototype can be found for this individual
in the Bible, his name, the role he plays, and his advice to Clay all suggest Hoffman's intention and focus. The character is the local judge in
Crowtown, Judge John Buskirk Montgomery. The name, of course, suggests "mountain," which in at least two of Hoffman's other novels symbolizes hope. In addition to the possible name symbolism of the judge,
he is quite clearly seen in the novel as a symbol of authority, and to Clay
himself he becomes a father figure; thoughts of the judge frequently re-
call to Clay's mind thoughts and sayings of his own long-dead father,
who had been a minister. On Clay's first visit to Judge Montgomery the
judge tells Clay, indirectly, that true salvation must come from the deed
and not the word: "'The greatest myth of all times is the Bible's Tower of
Babel. Communication is a snare and delusion. The failure of words is
indeed mankind's eternal curse'" (29).

But it is much later in the novel, in an obvious passage of hope for
the future, tinged with the poet's hope for the redemption and rebirth
suggested by spring, that the judge speaks most eloquently, not only
to Clay, but also to the reader. Shortly after Bea's departure, an unexpected encounter with Judge Montgomery points Clay to the road he
must take to achieve total completeness and redemption; it is election day in Crowtown, and the judge knows that he is on the way to
being voted out of office, for he has not succumbed to the guiles of
the political machine that controls the county. But even the defeated
judge has a vision and hope for the Clays of the world:

> "Winter's the best time in our mountains. All the wounds and
> scars are bandaged. I mourn for the mining of this people and this

6. 1 Kings 21:19–20.

land. Each year I give up hope, but then the good snows come, and the land is cleansed and sanctified. In the spring the earth will again try to bring forth fruit. Mostly it will be thistle and briar, but this earth will strive and perhaps, perhaps. . . .

"The wonder is they come back, the land and the people. In spite of abominations they do. Out of barrenness to budding, from budding to flower, and from flower to seed and the dropping of leaves to cover the next growth.

". . . What I'm trying to say is the earth is very forgiving. I believe it is attempting to teach us, to reveal a pattern and show us the way. . . .

"They claim there are no more frontiers in this country, this nation. I disagree. Morality's a new frontier. In my opinion it's our newest, or at least it's the oldest which has been forgotten and must be rediscovered. . . .

. . . "I shall attempt to simplify for you. . . . Sowing and reaping: those three words contain the wisdom of the ages. Everything is sowing and reaping." (218–19)

Transformed by Judge Montgomery's words, Clay resolves to free Vestil from his role as a male prostitute working on the third floor of the town's only hotel. Posing as a client in need of Vestil's services, Clay is ushered into the room by the unsuspecting "protector" of the house, Coon. From the moment Hoffman places Clay in room thirty-three, he increasingly identifies Clay with the Christ figure, one prepared to lay down his life for his fellow man, even for seemingly the least worthy of the lot. When Clay succeeds in giving Vestil a considerable sum of money to enable him to leave Crowtown and begin a new life somewhere else, Coon is ordered by the madame of the house to mutilate Clay:

"Do it!" she screamed.
"Going to!" Coon said. . . .
Coon rode him. A drop of powdery sweat fell from his chin onto Claytor's face. Claytor wept, whimpered, and retched. . . . Yet there was something else. . . .
The difference was that under all the riot of fear was a quietness, among all the terror a sureness, which he could only identify as something forming very much like courage. It found its way into his face, and he smiled—the bravest act of his life. . . .
A calmness and serenity flowed into him. He could have been dozing in the warmth of the summer sun. (242–43)

Clay is then allowed to leave the hotel, to bear perpetually the scars of his Calvary. And Hoffman reminds the reader of Christ's ascent as Clay makes his slow, painful journey to his home in the mountains:

> Snow fell faster.... Claytor swayed past mounds which were again clean.... A tipple appeared virginal. He left drops of blood in the snow. Wind blew flakes that like wafers settled on cinders....
> His blood sprinkled snow, the stains sinking like red seeds....
> Slowly he gathered his body to rise. He would climb to the house, clean himself, and meet them standing. (244–45)

Perhaps the clearest evidence of Hoffman's intention in *The Land That Drank the Rain* can be found in the book's title, and in a letter Hoffman wrote me in reply to my review of the novel. The source of the title is found in Hebrews 6:1–9: "For the earth which drinketh in the rain that cometh oft upon it, and bringeth forth herbs meet for them by whom it is dressed, receiveth blessing from God: But that which beareth thorns and briars is rejected, and is nigh unto cursing; whose end is to be burned." The chapter ends recalling God's promise to Abraham in Hebrews 6:15: "And so after he had patiently endured, he obtained the Promise."

Clay's ascent, the seasonal setting of the book from late fall through winter to the promise of spring, and the allusions and parallels already cited combine to show Hoffman's thematic intention: Redemption and salvation are always possible, but they can come only after expiation, contrition, and sacrifice. Finally, of my review, which had touched upon the "Christian theme of descent and ascension," Hoffman wrote:

> I did break a rule and read the review. I believe you have a fine understanding of what I attempted to do, and I know you would because of your theological background. My great worry is that most sophisticated people these days do not think morally or any other way.[7]

Godfires, Hoffman's ninth novel, continues the implicit examination of our degenerative society that started with *The Land That Drank the Rain.* In *Godfires,* however, the quest is skillfully hidden with one of the cleverest tales of detective fiction of the twentieth century. The reader is immediately plunged into an entertaining and frequently gripping double whodunit. First, who is the "Master" who has imprisoned and shackled Howell County's commonwealth attorney, Billy Payne, in a remote cabin deep in the recesses of a swamp and who returns almost daily to teach Billy about God, sin, expiation, grace, and

---

7. William Hoffman, letter to author, July 12, 1982.

forgiveness? Second, who is the slayer of Vincent Fallon Farr, one of the wealthiest and most influential citizens of Howell County, confidant of legislators and governors, and husband of the beautifully cultured, aristocratic, and striking Rhea Dillon Farr, with whom, incidentally, Billy has been in love all of his life?

For his setting for *Godfires* Hoffman returns to the land and people he knows so well. Thus the novel, although centered in Tobaccoton, Virginia, ranges from Richmond in the east to Lynchburg in the west, with other action and incidents occurring at nearby rural communities. The first-person point of view allows Hoffman to present the two concurrent plots already mentioned with an economy of language. All but one of the fifteen chapters that comprise the novel's over four hundred pages begin with an excerpt, usually brief, of the dialogue between Billy and the Master involving the religion lessons with which the Master is indoctrinating Billy.

The novel opens with a scene that can readily be seen in any one of the seemingly endless horror and sci-fi flicks that constitute the "in" movies of the 1980s: Billy Payne, the narrator-protagonist, is lying "belly down, . . . my chain clanking as I shift to gaze out the crooked doorway of the cabin toward motionless briars, tangled kudzu, and drooping swamp weed blooming yellow. I await the precise tread of the Master" (1). Hoffman then plays with the reader for over two hundred pages, describing "the Master" as an erect military figure who wears a Smith & Wesson .38 police special and a sheath knife "used to skin deer" (2).

There are many characters who play minor roles in *Godfires:* Florene Epes, Billy's secretary; Harrison Adams, a former silent business partner of the murdered Farr, who, not long before the discovery of Farr's body, had fought with him over a business venture gone sour; Doc Robinette, the small-town family physician and county medical examiner; Billy's father, an alcoholic so bent on reforming Billy that he pours vinegar into Billy's carefully hidden bourbon; and Sheriff Burton Pickney, one of Hoffman's finest portraits, a description of whom also conveys Hoffman's skill in using imagery:

> The sheriff sat at his oak desk, a man whose flesh was so loose it seemed the only thing holding him together was his rumpled tan uniform. Unbutton his shirt or drop his pants and he would've flowed across the floor like lard melting on a skillet. He moved no more than he had to, and when he had to, it was with a slow,

rolling gait, as if he perpetually paced the deck of a pitching ship
and needed to compensate for rough weather. (5)

But the most complete and most important character in the novel
other than Billy is Rhea, Vin Farr's widow, a beautiful and complex
woman haunted by ancestral pride always present in the massive
portrait of her mother that hangs in the living room of the Farr mansion. Rhea tells Billy that after the marriage with Vin had begun to
sour: "'I read a lot, even did a little private drinking, nothing like Vin's.
I'd sit in the quietness of the parlor sipping whiskey and looking at
my mother's portrait, trying to draw courage from her'" (282). Rhea,
cursed by the family pride she wears so proudly, laments, "I considered leaving him. I went to a Richmond lawyer, yet couldn't go
through with divorce because my mother would never have. I was a
Dillon woman. We won by lasting" (281).

The reader soon discovers that there are reasons for Rhea's fanati-
cism, both from the distant past, when as a young girl she discovered
an affair between her aristocratic father and one of his black farm-
workers, and from the present, her husband's multiple affairs with
local social friends of Rhea as well as with prostitutes from Richmond, including, as Billy later discovers, one special black prostitute
named Kitten, who talks only in rhymed couplets and who is well
equipped to offer special sexual favors to satisfy the most jaded and
degenerate of sexual appetites. But it was Vin himself who, trying to
force Rhea to play the same sexual games he played with his black
prostitutes in Richmond, slowly but surely began to write his own
death ticket.

But the "thrilling" aspect of the novel is merely Hoffman's framework that allows him to explore the real world of the eighties and
nineties, a Gothic inner world of mystery, spiritualism, illicit and
kinky sex, alcoholism, and most of all religion, especially hypocritical
religion. Billy himself describes Tobaccoton as "... tick-infested,
chigger-infested, but most of all ... religion-infested. If religion were
oak trees, we would've been living in a primeval forest instead of a
thirsting land where the red soil of fields flowed into the sun's glaze
like rivers of dust" (11).

The murder and its solution are only the background against which
Hoffman explores, reveals, and condemns the sick and diseased soci-
ety of big and small, urban and rural, late-twentieth-century America.
As Hoffman skillfully and adroitly plants clues along the way for both

Billy Payne and the reader, he is also simultaneously reminding us of the real problems of a materialistic world. By holding a mirror up to Billy and the others through the commentary of minor characters, Hoffman gives us the power that the poet Robert Burns pleaded for: to see ourselves as others see us. Thus we learn that Vincent Farr, as rich as he already was, still wanted more, and would run over whatever or whoever got in his way. Billy finds out this side of Vin when he talks with Harrison Adams, Vin's former business partner:

> ". . . Vin played it day by day. As long as things were going right, he was a perfect partner and never showed his tough side. It's just when a dollar bill's lying on the ground and you're stand- ing between him and it that he gets mean—or got mean."
>
> "I don't know what happens to people," Harrison said and ad- justed his cap. . . . "I been studying them a long time, and just when I think I'm beginning to understand something about human beings they change on me." (84)

Billy doesn't escape another disease of a sick society: a blindness to the worth of other people who just happen to be different, whether they are from "the other side of the tracks," are less fortunate, or are simply black. As Leona Poindexter and Billy's own faithful and loyal housekeeper, Aunt Lettie, speak to him about his ignoring of blacks in general, Billy and the reader realize that he is as guilty of a lack of compassion and understanding as Mildred Douglas is contemptuous of Yank in Eugene O'Neill's *The Hairy Ape*. Billy has gone to Richmond to see if the daughter of Ben, Rhea's black gardener who has not been seen since Vin's death, knows where her father is hiding. After Leona tells Billy that her father is not hiding, but has come to Richmond to visit her, she takes offense at Billy's statement that he has always liked Ben:

> "Known him most your life?" she asked. "Been intimately asso- ciated with him? You ever sat down beside him to break bread, of- fered him a cigarette, sent him a Christmas card?"
>
> "No, but I have a genuinely good feeling for Ben and believed it to be reciprocated."
>
> "Sure, Daddy knows how to do up white folks. He takes off his hat and bows. They think what a cute little darky he is. I tell you something. My father reads Plato. He's read the complete works of Plato. How many people in Howell County ever heard of Plato? They's think you mean Mickey Mouse's dog." (182)

Godfires, then, continues the scrutiny of a society and a world that Hoffman began to explore in earnest with *The Land That Drank the Rain.* Some of the same themes from that work are carried into *Godfires*—private sin, jaded sex, bonded prostitution—but others, equally damning to the individual as well as to the society to which he belongs, are added, notably the frenzied twentieth-century pursuit of money and of power and influence that follow, the dangers of hypocritical and obsessive religion, and prejudice toward other fellow humans, either of a different lifestyle such as that of the hippies encountered or of another race, whether consciously or unconsciously ridiculed or ignored.

In an accompanying essay in this collection, Jeanne Nostrandt discusses with considerable skill Hoffman's tenth novel, *Furors Die.* The casual reader of this novel is unaware of a link between its themes and its dedication, but to close friends of Bill Hoffman it will come as no surprise that the novel is dedicated to Hoffman's former minister and to his wife. In his writing, Hoffman has always been interested in questions of a moral, theological, or philosophical nature: One recalls immediately Tod Young of *Yellow Leaf,* Jackson LeJohn of *A Walk to the River,* Claytor Carson of *The Land That Drank the Rain,* and Billy Payne of *Godfires.* But another reason for such a dedication—apart from a firm and long-lasting friendship—is that *Furors Die* can be read as a parable on the seven deadly sins, with special emphasis on pride, avarice, and lust.

The story is essentially a rich and detailed account of the growing up and coming of age of its two main characters, Wylie Duval and Amos "Pinky" Cody. Wylie has it all, and at an early age: new cars, easy girls, and a free-swinging country club lifestyle. Pinky, on the other hand, is overly influenced by a frenzied and aggressive mother, a member of a Pentecostal religious sect; Pinky outwardly chastises and condemns everything that Wylie represents, yet he inwardly envies Wylie's youthful boozing and sexual liberty. Without contriving incidents or encounters, Hoffman skillfully weaves a plot that keeps the two lives constantly in focus, so that the reader discovers the gradual weighing and shifting of values on the part of Pinky, and Wylie's attempts to dissociate himself from Pinky.

Because Pinky worked through high school as an office boy for Wylie's highly successful father, and especially because Pinky had talked a frustrated and slightly deranged tenant out of holding Wylie's father as a hostage, Mr. Duval sends Pinky to Wylie's prep school, White Oak, in Virginia, expecting and demanding that Wylie "look after Pinky." Although Wylie bitterly resents the situation, to retain his father's goodwill and financial support he reluctantly agrees to his father's request, thus bringing the two boys into a relationship that allows the seed of future discord to take deep root.

There are no heroes in this novel, at least not in the contemporary sense of the term. Neither Wylie nor Pinky can really understand each other, and neither makes any solid attempt to try. For example, on the occasion of the death of Pinky's father, an event that went unnoticed by Wylie for several months, Wylie, following a chance encounter with Pinky, tells him "'I'm so damn sorry,'" to which Pinky, summing up Wylie's attitude and concern in a single striking sentence, replies, "'Not really. You want to be because that's the correct attitude, but you never knew my father and never cared to. . . . He didn't have the grace and style you find as necessary as air . . . in all the years since White Oak, you've never once asked about him—whether he was dead or alive'" (208).

And yet Wylie, at least on the surface and to those who know him, is not an evil person. In the best tradition of the so-called southern gentleman he is a well-mannered, sociable, highly successful businessman, regular in his attendance at church, a better-than-average tennis player, a generous husband. But like too many in a materialistic, yuppie society, Wylie lacks a proper sense of values, of morals. As one of his sexual conquests, Trish, tells him, "'We're not moral people. . . . [I]t's not your moral code that's hurt, it's your pride'" (154). Pride, covetousness, anger, and lust are omnipresent in this novel, with almost every character, major and minor, afflicted with each vice to varying degrees. Ultimately, however, *Furors Die* is not only a parable on the seven deadly sins; it is also, and perhaps primarily, a satire on a greedy, materialistic, mechanistic, and sick society—a society, Hoffman warns, as doomed as the grand schemes and airy monuments built by both the Wylies and the Pinkys of our world.

What, then, is the place of William Hoffman in contemporary American literature, and especially in southern literature? One can begin by claiming for him a range and a richness that few of his contemporaries possess: Whether Hoffman is writing of the horrors of World War II or of the permanent scars inflicted by war both on its participants as well as on those who stand and wait, his words and images touch our raw nerves and make us blink, wince, or cry. But, as with all gifted and talented writers, the themes of Hoffman's fiction are what will endure. His subjects, in the course of a novel, become themes: honor, courage, love, self-sacrifice, war, the struggle to survive, and the southern agrarian theme of the rape of the land. Taken together, these eleven novels comprise one writer's spiritual quest throughout the second half of the twentieth century.

A Life without End
Two Novels about World War II by William Hoffman

George Garrett

▬▬ ▬ ▬▬ ▬▬

> The Army was becoming a life without
> end. We would always be at war.

> —*Yancey's War*

In the years following World War II there were any number of out-standing fiction works that were set historically in the war and, at least in part, inspired by a desire to bring home the hard truths of the war as witnessed and experienced by its participants. These were called "war novels," as if they were a kind of genre like thrillers and westerns and romances. Some of these, like John Hersey's *A Bell for Adano* and Harry Brown's *A Walk in the Sun* were trailblazers in that they appeared early, while the war was still in progress. Of course these early versions, honest and critical as they could be, were partly conditioned, if not controlled, by the rules of home-front censorship at the time (an aspect of those times not often remembered nowa-days) and even by paper rationing, which determined to an extent the length of books and the size of printings. Hersey and Brown and others were honest to a fault, but all of them were part of the war ef-fort. They knew more than they could ever say. In depicting the gritty reality and absurdity of war, no fiction at the time even came close to the cartoons of Bill Mauldin, a veteran of the Forty-fifth Infantry Division, whose newspaper cartoons were published in book form (entitled *Up Front*) in 1945. They were part and parcel of the war ef-fort also, though not all the army brass viewed them that way. In an early cartoon, "Willie" and "Joe," ragged and bestubbled and sitting together on a rocky Italian hillside near a dead tree, leisurely digging a foxhole with their inadequate entrenching tools, M-1 rifles leaning against the trunk of the dead tree, speak to and for all the writers who followed. Willie is saying: "You'll get over it, Joe. Oncet I wuz gonna write a book exposin' the army after th' war myself."

In the years immediately following the war, and continuing on into the 1960s—thus written and published with first the Korean War and then the Vietnam War serving as both background and refresher course—there were a lot of war novels, mainly dealing with World

War II, written by Americans and for Americans. European war novels, including those by British writers, though treating the same experience, by and large had a different stance. Perhaps because the war was much longer for them and was fought on home ground, meaning that the civilian population was essentially in the front lines, their point of view was not an end to innocence. Instead, it is characterized by an overwhelming weariness and a despair born of the indifference that tormented the survivors. Something of this attitude can be seen in a major work of autobiographical nonfiction, *All the Brave Promises,* by American novelist Mary Lee Settle. Having served in the British WAAF, her account offers the innocence at the outset, "when we were young, dashing and lively," as well as the weight of shrugging indifference at the end when "the juggernaut of war . . . was spending itself toward its own death like a great tiring unled beast."[1]

Some of the good American war novels, ones that have stood the test of time, are books like John Horne Burns's *The Gallery;* Norman Mailer's *The Naked and the Dead;* James Gould Cozzens's prizewinning *Guard of Honor;* Paxton Davis's *Two Soldiers;* James Jones's *From Here to Eternity* (as well as the rest of the trilogy on which he worked his whole life, including *The Thin Red Line* and *Whistle*); Joseph Heller's *Catch-22;* Kurt Vonnegut's *Slaughterhouse Five;* and others. J. D. Salinger is (reliably) reported to have written a large war novel that, in the end, he scrapped, keeping only the opening and closing scenes that became the superb short story "For Esme with Love and Squalor." In between those two scenes the war is implied, so that the war becomes anything you can imagine—everyman's war novel. One of our greatest postwar writers, Shelby Foote, a World War II veteran in both the U.S. Army and the Marine Corps, set his war novel, *Shiloh,* during the Civil War. It is essentially "in costume," a kind of reenactment before that was a habit. Similarly, Stephen Becker, though he has written novels based on his Marine Corps experiences in China, set his principal war novel during the Civil War—*When the War Is Over.*

I mention all these good books, some of them justly renowned, because William Hoffman's two novels dealing directly with World War II unquestionably belong in their company and at the highest rank of the American fiction coming out of World War II.

1. Mary Lee Settle, *All the Brave Promises: Memoirs of an Aircraft Woman Second Class* (New York: Delacorte, 1976), 176.

The first of these was Hoffman's first published novel, *The Trumpet Unblown* (1955), which follows the adventures and misadventures of a young Virginia private, Tyree Shelby, from the time he joins his out-fit, a field hospital unit in England, through the invasion of Normandy and the rest of the war until his return home. Hoffman's publisher, Doubleday, evidently wishing to emphasize authenticity, accuracy, and, to an extent, its autobiographical elements, announced on the book jacket that it is "A Novel of the Medical Corps in World War II," and stressed the author's personal experience of the war: "William Hoffman made the invasion of Europe on D-plus-3 with the 91st Evacuation Hospital." Told in a straightforward third-person narra-tive with young and inexperienced Shelby as the center of conscious-ness, the story moves, as the war itself does, steadily and inexorably from what might now be called "a bad scene" at the outset to the hal-lucinatory edges of nightmare, staggering finally to an ending when, unable to communicate with his parents and his fiancée, Cotton, un-able to begin to tell them what he (and the reader following him like a shadow throughout) has seen and felt, done and left undone, blurts out some truths in a final moment with Cotton, truths that we know are abstracted from the unspeakable context of the war:

> "What is it, Ty?" she asked, leaning against him.
> "I don't know. Just about everything I guess."
> "You never answered my question."
> "What question?"
> "Don't you like me any longer?" she asked, putting her fine arms around him.
> Shelby looked at her, and for a moment he was tempted. Then very precisely he took her arms from around himself and laid her hands in her lap.
> "You wouldn't want to kiss a fellow that's had gonorrhea, would you?"
> Her eyes widened.
> "A fellow who's been in the nut ward of a hospital and should have been in prison?"
> "Please, Ty."
> "That isn't all. A fellow who's lived with a kraut whore and been a coward."
> She stared at him.
> "There's a couple more minor things. A fellow who's lied, cheated, murdered, and just about anything else left in the book."
> She sat staring at him until water filled her eyes, then bent her head to her hands and cried softly. He did not move. He watched

her cry, and he watched them dancing and laughing under the
colored lights.

"I'll take you home," he said to Cotton when she finished crying.

"I don't care, Ty," she said, wiping her eyes.

"You care."

"You're just hurt. It'll get all right."

"I'm afraid not."

"I'll keep on. If you want to, I'll keep on."

"Would you?"

"Yes, if you want to."

As he watched her he filled up inside. He wanted to touch her
hair and make believe it could be. But this one last thing he could
do right. This he would do for her.

"That's just the point," he lied. "I don't want to." (303–4)

Thus Shelby's final act, his first moral act since war experience
stunned and corrupted him (and everyone else in the unit and the
story), is, in fact, to tell a lie.

The novel is quick-moving and relatively short; it is at times laconic.
The limits of Shelby's consciousness and point of view work well, for
he is an engaging character, an innocent, to be sure, unsophisticated
and immature. But he possesses a strength of character, a physical
toughness, and a strong sense of honor; he is easily established as a
reliable witness. Through him we gradually come to know the others
in the unit, mostly veterans of the earlier campaign in North Africa,
restlessly awaiting the war's next stage, the invasion, to begin. To an
experienced eye, the unit from the beginning would appear to be out
of control, rapidly deteriorating and disintegrating; but from the point
of view of the young volunteer, it may be strange, unexpected, but still
simply the way things are. What we have is a classic "straight man" in
a surreal, comedic (if dangerous) situation. Shelby is kept busy basi-
cally fighting for his life and honor against a savage, sadistic brute
named Blizzard. We get to know the others in the outfit, including the
amazing Petras, called the Greek, who is obviously a precursor of
some of the characters in *Catch-22* and (later) *M*A*S*H*, a hustler and
a fixer who can somehow arrange everything.

Suddenly all this life comes to an end as the unit is alerted, packed
up, and shipped off to be part of the invasion:

Colonel Harlan spoke well. He told them the record of the out-
fit was unparalleled in the ETO and that the most glorious chapters were yet to be written. He told them how proud he was to

serve with them. They had had a good and deserved rest, he said, but now it was time to get down to business and their business was war. He told them a training schedule would appear and that he expected all noncoms to whip their sections into keen functioning. Then Colonel Harlan closed his speech with a prayer. The last words were, "May God give us the victory." (84)

Once landed, amid chaos and confusion, lost stores and missing personnel, they find a place to set up the field hospital and to be about their business of war. Nothing goes quite as Shelby had imagined it and not quite as most readers will have imagined or even experienced it, either:

> Surgery was a butcher shop in which doctors worked without gowns and let sterile technique go, cutting and sawing with sweat pouring over their skin. Metal drums were put by the tables to receive the lopped-off arms and legs. The drums were always overflowing. (117)

And, as horror and exhaustion wear down Shelby, it grows worse:

> It became a nightmare in which there was no time or reason. Death piled higher and higher, and the world became a place of stumps and torn intestines, of gangrene and men without faces, of giving plasma to men burned crisp like bacon, whose veins were almost impossible to find under the stinking black flesh, of using suction machines to keep the tracheotomy cases from drowning in their own spit, and Ward 4 sounded as if it were full of vipers from the air hissing between the little metal buttons in their throats. (118)

This is the business of war, pages of it, as no one else has presented it—head-on, unflinching. Soon, in spite of his shock and fatigue, Shelby becomes fascinated with his job which, in the confusion, has expanded: "Shelby found himself performing duties that belonged rightfully only to doctors and nurses. Someone had to do them" (120). He begins to study what is going on all around him when he has a chance and time:

> He had held the popular idea that surgery was a very fine and precise affair, but the first thing that struck him was how brutal it was. The patients were sawed, hammered, hacked, and wrestled

on the tables. When a femur was being set, the patient was thrown around like a side of beef on the block, the doctors and nurses tugging and cursing like roustabouts. He soon lost his civilian's awe of doctoring. (125)

Soon enough everything is routine. The field hospital follows the killing, moves forward and sets up to "wait for the flesh to come in." The war continues, their lives becoming more and more routine. Some of the soldiers go into Paris for drinks and whores and Shelby loses his virginity. By fits and starts, and with a gradually more evident moral decay, the unit moves back and forth in France, Belgium, Holland; the Battle of the Bulge comes and goes. They come and go and end the war in Germany on the banks of the Elbe.

The inner life of Shelby and the others is deftly summoned and revealed by a whole series of almost surreal events—thievery, rape, murder, betrayals, some of them grotesquely comic—as the men in the unit shed the last vestiges of whatever civilization they had acquired before the war. Long before the war's end we are at home in a world where the absurdities recounted in *Catch-22* would seem completely logical and fairly mild. One by one the people in the outfit, those whom we know through Shelby, disappear or come to bad ends. It is peace that breaks each of them. Shelby finally cracks up, too, is taken to a hospital and shortly thereafter is sent back to the United States where he is almost lost among those he loved. He imagines telling the truth to his parents: "'When I look at you and everyone I see your intestines and smell the way you would stink with gangrene and can never forget how pitiful you and I really are or how easily we can be broken into nothing'" (299).

The Trumpet Unblown is a brilliant and passionate book, certainly one of the finest of the novels to come out of World War II. In design and in all the small details it is superbly crafted, magnificently written. Part of its power comes from the fact that both its passion and its brilliance are tightly reined in, held in check. The style, sentence by sentence, is matter of fact, direct, transparent even when dealing with the most extraordinary events and circumstances. The tension created by the contrast between the calm voice and its terrible tales makes the impact on the reader all the more powerful. The abrupt shifts from all kinds of comedy to horror and back make both these qualities more emphatic and make the experience more rounded and complex.

In *The Trumpet Unblown* William Hoffman proved himself once and for all a major writer with the touch and judgment of a master. That it is not better known, that it was not honored in its first brief season must be attributable to the terrible truths it shows and tells.

A little more than a decade later, with several novels and many short stories behind him, William Hoffman returned to the times and the setting of World War II with *Yancey's War* (1966). This novel is, it seems, a different kind of war novel in many ways. Almost three-quarters of the story takes place at home, on "the home front," accurately evoked; and it concerns in some detail the ups and downs of basic training, Officer Candidate School, and the haphazard, not to say hopeless, training of "the Golden Eagles." They are a pathetic infantry regiment, which, in one of the great, extended, laugh-out-loud comic sequences in our literature, has trouble enough surviving on maneuvers and proves itself to be clearly worthless as a potential combat unit. Eventually even the U.S. Army is able to figure this out, and in England, prior to the invasion, the regiment is broken up; all that remains becomes a laundry unit whose basic duties should keep it far from any front-line action. Unfortunately, near the end of the war in Germany, a simple mistake (not the first, by any means) in map reading puts the unit in a town where its members are ambushed and forced to fight for their lives against serious odds.

This section is brief, sudden, and brutal—just like combat; in spite of various absurdities, it is not the least bit funny. After a long, steady build-up, during which there is a long wait for the American G.I.'s, there is suddenly enough war to last the survivors for a lifetime. There are even moments of credible heroism by these very unheroic men. All that has happened before, all that led them this far, is meaningless, wiped out. It all comes down to a confused and desperate firefight in a few hours in a strange place.

This is high-risk storytelling, designed to dramatize an essential if often unspoken truth about war: that in those moments when all the things that have been imagined, feared, and trained and prepared for, however ineptly, do come to pass, there is nothing else that matters. Paradoxically, in a larger sense that no common soldier in the midst of things can conceive of, these terrible moments of truth do not matter, either. Thus, although it means everything to them, nothing that happens to the unlucky and incompetent laundrymen or their German enemies—a mixture of home guard, young and old, and of implacable SS—has any significance for the war itself. For all practical purposes the war is already over as they are fighting one another to the death.

To tell this story, making all the parts of it authentic and meaningful (even if the deepest meaning is that it all meant next to nothing) required the highest kind of virtuosity. James Jones had used a somewhat similar strategy in *From Here to Eternity,* devoting the largest part of this story to the peacetime army and its life and problems, all of which vanish or are transformed by the completely unexpected event of the Japanese attack on Pearl Harbor. But Jones's story becomes, for the most part, a more traditional story of initiation. Hoffman's story does not contrast America at peace and at war—we are already in the war on page one—but makes the case, in *this* case at least, that there is nothing that can be prepared for and nothing that anyone can be initiated into. Everything comes down to luck and death. "The big picture," much invoked by the army as the place where all the details come together in some meaningful pattern, does not exist. The results are comedy, when nobody really is hurt, as in the disastrous maneuvering, and tragedy without benefit of catharsis, as Hoffman's characters live and die in acts of war. Luck and death, the final products of *Yancey's War,* go well beyond the stunned pity and pathos at the heart of *The Trumpet Unblown.*

In a literary sense, as a matter of storytelling, *Yancey's War* is more complex and more layered in ambiguities as well. The central story is the gradual unveiling and exposure of the life of Marvin Yancey (born Yankovitch), a middle-aged, well-to-do veteran of World War I, and a decorated hero from that war, who turns out to be something more and a lot less than he seems to be. He is a mysterious figure, if fat and often foolish. Throughout the story there are disclosures and surprises about Yancey. For example, it turns out that although his medals from World War I are real, the acts of heroism for which he is credited were not. Similarly, at the end of things, Yancey performs an act of extraordinary heroism, which costs him his life, mainly motivated by overwhelming fear and cowardice. At the naked moment of truth he becomes a hero only because there is no other choice left for him.

This is complicated, fully dimensional material. It is made more complex and ambiguous because our sole source of information and judgment concerning Yancey is the first-person narrator, young Charles

Elgar, of a good old family in Richmond. Elgar has been aptly described by editor and critic George Core as "sophisticated, ironic, and world-weary," to which should be added the adjective *unreliable*. It is not that Elgar is not trustworthy; he is engaging and easy, at least at first, to identify with. Yancey, seen through his eyes, is a crude, manipulative clown, unforgettable only in his vulgarity and folly. Very gradually, however, without diminishing the validity of Elgar's picture of Yancey, we come to recognize serious flaws in Elgar's character as, motivated as much by revenge as anything else, he does things, including the seduction of Yancey's attractive wife, that render his role as our guide and moral arbiter somewhat suspect. It is not so much that Elgar's perceptions and judgments are *wrong*—by and large they are acceptable. What is demonstrated is that none of our perceptions and judgments of other human beings, no matter what their source, are good enough. There is always more than we can know. Both Elgar and Yancey perform bravely and are duly awarded medals—Yancey's posthumously—for their bravery. But a point not quite lost on Elgar is that Yancey's cowardly first reaction, that they should surrender to the Germans, is in fact the course of wisdom and would have saved many lives on both sides. Elgar acts on the perception, which proves to be wrong, that the Germans have executed those of their men who have already surrendered during the ambush. Elgar's excellent leadership and undeniable courage prove to be totally unnecessary. This kind of narration has all the subtlety and power of Joseph Conrad or Henry James at their best and finest.

The two books, taken together, have a curious relationship. They are companion stories, each in a sense needing the other for the whole story of the war. There is a little moment in *Yancey's War* when the laundry unit briefly shares some space with a field hospital, probably the one from *The Trumpet Unblown*. They touch on one another and go on about their business and their separate dooms. In terms of action and event the earlier novel is more shocking in its initial impact. Surely the physical horrors of war and its effects have seldom, if ever, been more directly and vividly described. But, curiously, it is not a world without hope. In *Yancey's War,* the world is intrinsically beyond our understanding and, except for brief delusions, is a hopeless place.

Taken together, Hoffman's two war novels are a remarkable achievement, a full and sufficient statement about World War II from the point of view of a gifted writer who has experienced it and in time comes to understand it, including his understanding of the limits of knowing and judging. These are important books, then, among the finest of our time. Even in a world with only illusory hopes, one may be allowed to wish that these books will last for as long as books and stories of our times may matter.

Mary Poppins's Mouth

Dabney Stuart

For most of his fiction—at this writing, eleven novels and four collections of stories since *The Trumpet Unblown* appeared in 1955—William Hoffman uses three principal locations: Richmond, Virginia, and its surroundings; Farmville and Prince Edward County, which he calls Tobaccoton (and, in *A Walk to the River,* Black Leaf), about seventy miles southwest of Richmond; and eastern West Virginia, focusing on Charleston and a composite coal-mining area. He sets *A Death of Dreams* (1973; his seventh novel) in the first of these, until the final seventeen pages when Guy Dion makes his way into the ruins of Boone, a once prosperous mining town. Although Hoffman places Boone in western Virginia, it is interchangeable with the West Virginia mining areas central to novels such as *The Dark Mountains* (1963) and *Furors Die* (1990).

Under pressure from his wife, Lucy, and daughter, Dibs, Guy Dion has taken his doctor's advice and checked himself into Westview, a hospital in a rural area, an hour's drive across the James River on Route 60 west of Richmond. Westview is a drying-out facility for alcoholics of various stripes, although we figure this out a good deal sooner than Dion does. An aspect of the novel's concern is Guy's denial of his condition, and part of Hoffman's achievement is the skill with which he paces Guy's gradual discovery and admission of where his life has brought him. Very little "happens" beyond this, in fact, until Guy's escape roughly five-sixths of the way through, yet the novel is filled with activity minutely and shrewdly observed. It is a paradigm of the individual psyche's slow opening to the inexorable impingements of the world external to it, and to its own hidden past, a movement toward identification and limits.

Apparently in late middle age, Dion is the successful chief executive of Old Virginia Communications and Research, a firm he helped found as a young man, after a job with AT&T. The company's "two-tiered electric" (10) sign rises high above the James River in the downtown Richmond skyline, a sign that Guy takes as the flag of his true country. His allegiance to that country has, however, emptied him and driven him to the bottle.

As the existence of the hospital and its considerable population makes clear, Dion's case is anything but isolated. Twenty-six other patients have roles of varying importance as Hoffman builds the daily routine of the hospital. All of them are casualties of the Rich-mond world of big business and finance. Mayben, a scion of the family of an importer, suffers from masochism internalized from his father's abusing him, which he has come to believe he deserves; Carwyle is an illustrious attorney until, nude, he greets Girl Scouts selling cookies at his front door; Casto, a real-estate broker, drives his Coup-de-Ville through the plate-glass front of an A&P. There are also, among others, a minister, a banker, a Pulitzer Prize–winning journalist, a politician, and a former child actor. The list is a coherent documentation of the cost of position and affluence, earned or inherited, and the novel itself acts in part as a sociology of the city's upper crust.

The ravages of the spirit and integrity of its members are not restricted to the patients in the hospital, either. Guy Dion's daughter, for example, is divorced, homeless, and herself a closet drinker; his colleagues are grasping and treacherous. There may be healthy entrepreneurs and lawyers and investment figures in Richmond's wealthy circles, but they make no appearances in this book.

These people are characters in the traditional sense of that term— a cast of allusions to areas of life with which readers can be assumed to be familiar, verbal evocations of behavior we can be expected to complete and recognize—and they help adumbrate a social determinism, but Hoffman uses them as principles of the book's structure as well.[1] This is essential in a novel not driven (until very late) by plot, but by pressure toward psychic illumination. There is a series of dining-hall scenes in which the conversations (or rather counterpointed verbal blurts sometimes sequential, sometimes not) expand one's sense of the workings of the hospital while signaling states in Guy's growing awareness of his condition and what he needs to do to get out—in other words, the development of a patient's local mentality, his adaptation. In this progression three of the other patients (two old friends of Guy's, another indication of the small circle of his world) become instruments in the narrative: Cooley embodies a positive and seriocomic model for biding one's time until the right moment; Barney Moon acts as a negative instance of self-defeating aggression and psychic arrest; and Montjoy, the gastronomic preacher, affords the crux on which Hoffman turns both Dion's dis-

1. I mean this poor, flogged word only in a broad architectural sense: The novel has parts that are intentionally related to each other and compose a harmonious and purposeful whole.

covery about himself and the mode of the novel's momentum. Taken together, the three characters aim at, and in Cooley's case facilitate, Guy's eventual escape from the hospital.

Hoffman further controls the novel's shape and development through carefully placed visits from the world outside the hospital: Guy's wife, Lucy; then Lucy, Dibs, and his two grandchildren; and finally, to signal the continuing importance of his business, a colleague, Bart Brevet, whom Guy considers his protégé and lone remaining ally. Counterpointed with these visits are Guy's own conferences with the three doctors who preside over the institution. He meets with them first in ascending order of their importance in the organization and is frustrated in all cases, especially in his final session with Dr. Cletus, during which, through Cletus's stereotype misprision of Guy's homosexual encounter with Montjoy, Hoffman gives his narrative its most surprising and, I think, brilliant shift.

This pattern of character as structural device extends into the use of the hospital staff, and expands with instances of Guy's past asserting itself, particularly his memory of an early love, Lotte, who rejected his marriage proposal. The five-chapter section (38–42) that culminates in his meeting with Lotte in the women's Annex gazebo is a story in itself, both baffling the novel's progression with its occurrence, and, along with Montjoy's behavior in the next chapter (43), releasing Guy from his frozen self-deception, and the narrative from the locus of the hospital.

Overarching all these instances—giving them, as it were, room in which to accomplish their complex counterpoint and entwinements— is Hoffman's management of time. In *A Death of Dreams* he employs a technique similar to Thomas Mann's in *The Magic Mountain*. He records the days and their patterns exactly for slightly over half the novel, the first seven full days of Guy Dion's sojourn at the hospital, the week of biblical creation, the mystical seven so important to ritual. Then in less than thirty pages the next ten days slip by, notched infrequently on the novel's calendar. In the final fourteen chapters—the focus on Lotte is the fulcrum here, too—the tracking of time disappears altogether (though days are named) and it is with considerable surprise that we learn after his escape that Guy's time as a patient has extended beyond two months.[2]

2. Cf. p. 304: DeWitt says, "Your medical insurance ran out. It covers only 60 days." This recalls, painfully, Lucy's first visit to Westview, where the following exchange took place:

We lose track of Guy's stay; so does he, which is the point. He begins to be as entangled in his life at the hospital as he had been in the life that brought him there. This shift coincides with his discovery of Lotte's presence at the Annex (hinted at as early as chapter 18), and the narrative's gradual turn toward less radial and more linear progression, showing Hoffman's skill at bringing into compressed focus a number of heretofore disparate motifs—memory; search and discovery; sexual desire and frustration; his fine sense of when to alter pace over the course of a long book; his ability to bring what has been on the novel's outskirts to its center smoothly and economically. It also focuses on one of the basic dreams that has died, long before Guy Dion was brought to his alcoholic impasse that is the novel's superficial impetus: his loss of Lotte and the image of life that he projected with her.

It has not died altogether, of course, but has gone underground, snaking its way through the consequent decisions composing Guy's life: his marriage to Lucy, his commitment to his company, the raising of his children. These are among the most basic and honorable human pursuits, but in giving himself to them Guy has repressed his real self; he has substituted accommodations and compromises for it over the decades, taking the subsequent illusion for substance. Psychologically speaking, reality catches up with him when he meets Lotte in the gazebo. Formally speaking, the insistent pattern of images of Lotte from the past that Hoffman has woven into Guy's mental life at the hospital reaches its fruition in this incident. Psychological and formal patterns, then, complement one another, merging into clarity at this point. Given this development, the novel's pace and style—though not its central preoccupation—and Guy's mode of behavior, *have* to change.

Before I attend in more detail to the phases of Guy's psychological development that come to a climax in his meeting with Lotte, I want to note how adroitly Hoffman presents the shifting distinction between subjective and external truth in the life at the hospital, and the incremental use he makes of it.

"Do they [Guy's colleagues] think I'm a drunk?"

"Oh no."

"I've seen men go away. They disappear from the club for a month or six weeks. They return pale and haunted looking."

"You're not one of those." (133)

First, it is only through piecing together suggestion and innuendo that one knows the institution is for people who are victims of what today is termed alcohol abuse. The facility is called only Westview (it is also often referred to as "the mansion") and not until after Guy escapes from it does he confront his illness.

The fictional point of view—any novel's hub—focuses on this illness continually. Hoffman limits his third-person narrator to Guy Dion's physical and mental presence. Guy's persistent attitude while he is interned is that he is not sick, but is quite normal. His first day barely begins—he arrives toward noon on a Thursday—before he is demanding to see the doctor so he can go home. This denial continues until his assignation with Lotte. Since we are limited to Guy's perspective, our understanding of his predicament is filtered through his; the primary implication is that he *is* normal, there *has* been a mistake: the hospital is for sick people among whom he is out of place.

But it is countered from various angles. Bailey, one of the patients at Guy's dining table, spots his trouble immediately at lunch on Guy's first day. After some distinguishing remarks from other patients at the table, Bailey, silent until then, says, "'How would you like a cold, very dry martini right this moment?'" (33). Bailey persists over the ensuing week: Each time he brings up the "shimmering idea" of a drink, Guy is unable to push it from his mind. He also has trouble eating, which Bailey's insinuations exacerbate.

Hoffman uses another of the patients, Sickles, to similar effect, his knowing reaction suggesting he sees what Bailey sees (78). Lucy's and Guy's colleague's refusal to honor his request to come home further indicates that the consistent narrative emphasis is partly a formal equipoise to Guy's denial of his condition, as do the predictable reactions of the various physicians he talks to.

The way Hoffman presents these consultations complicates the tension between Guy's subjective attitude and the external implications contrary to it. During the first few days Guy Dion sees and hears things that puzzle him: "scuffling" in the darkness (64), a scream in the night (65), and a hearse bearing away a body from the rear entrance during Quiet Hour (114). When he attempts to discuss these events first with Dr. Bertie (90ff) and later with Dr. Cletus (137ff), the doctors uniformly deny them. The physicians' denials suggest bureaucratic obfuscation; when we learn that the thumping sounds Guy hears at night are Chuck's working with barbells, Guy's credibility seems verified and the impression of cover-up even more likely.

To confuse matters further, in these interviews Hoffman has the doctors raise the occurrences of Guy's sexual advances toward certain female employees: Miss Ailey, the activities coordinator (41); Miss Williams, the night nurse (twice: 63 and 151); and Miss Amos, another nurse (108–9), before whom he stands naked. The doctors present the first three of these instances—all of which we have "witnessed"—accurately. Guy has indeed made the gestures referred to; he is responsible. *Some* of the doctors' statements are confirmed; their professional dependability seems at least partially restored. This plausibility, however, is undercut when they patently misinterpret the fourth incident, Guy's allegedly exhibiting himself to Miss Amos.

One of the main external sources of information about Guy's condition, then, which would seem at first to offer a reputable corroboration of Guy's illness, is itself called into question by the physicians' own subjective clinical predispositions, and their self-interest and power, characteristics given their fullest expression in Dr. Cletus's smug, laughably misguided interpretation of the Montjoy episode, in chapter 44.

Guy *does* have a drinking problem that has incapacitated him, of course. That's clear after his binge with Barney Moon in chapter 31, but Hoffman has established the novel's terms and direction substantially by then. Hoffman's intention is, I think, to generate a familiar setup initially, only to move beyond it into richer, more fundamentally revealing areas. It appears at first that we are dealing with a straightforward story of a man denying his illness, plunged into a tussle with an institution that seeks to cure him. Hoffman uses the narrative voice, as I have suggested, to help create that temporary tension. But as the institution is undermined, the poles of the struggle shift. The tension between the subjective and external becomes instead tension between aspects of the subjective; the struggle within Guy Dion's psyche emerges as the substratum and true subject of the novel. As it takes the narrative time to break through the superficies of the institution's involvement, so it takes Dion time to discover his real predicament. The relatively simple distinction between subjective and external undergoes a radical dissolution into the infinitely more problematical disharmony of the individual self.

From a perspective that seeks to unite the psychological and formal aspects of the novel, one could say as well that the narrative voice is finally more concerned with Guy Dion's cure than is the institution to which he has been semivoluntarily committed. This is as it should be.

The institution's flaws, which are human and not affectionately satirized by Hoffman (Barney Moon says, "'Doctors have no honor'" [176], and nothing in this novel contradicts that judgment), render it incapable of helping Guy Dion. He must use his circumstances—including the ineffectual nature of the hospital, which becomes part of his opportunity—to help himself. The narrative structure implies what is eventually articulated dramatically: help is internal; it may be sought from the buried past; it requires the subtle, long-term labor of stripping away one's persona.

The struggle, then, is not between Guy Dion's version of the truth and the institution's version of it, which are only so many flawed, partial human perspectives at loggerheads with each other. The more basic struggle occurs among aspects of Guy's personality, the needs of the self as opposed to the requirements it internalizes from without: expectations of family and other forms through which society seeks to perpetuate itself. William Hoffman sides with the isolate individual against whose integrity the odds are majestically stacked, and because of that imbalance of circumstance the individual becomes more courageously determined and is therefore more worthy of admiration and respect.

There is a sometimes excruciatingly poignant, sometimes humorous, side to this predicament that accompanies the attempt to institutionalize the psychic care of disparate identities. The other patients sharing Guy Dion's experience in the hospital Hoffman treats with the affection and dignity he withholds from the doctors. With Guy's more elaborately drawn difficulties, they compose a group in whose strange and heartrending woundings Hoffman's sympathies ground themselves. Some of the scenes—often only the most fleeting tableaux—are as eerily memorable as any in literature. The extent of life's exactions from these characters is exorbitant, yet none of them has given up.

Montjoy, for example, though by now a career patient, attempts to sustain his illusion that he's a functioning clergyman. He runs Sunday "services" at the hospital chapel: grape juice for Christ's blood, and for his body Rainbow bread scooped from the loaf with a miniature melon dicer. The service is a testy crosswind of existential theological views spouted by the few attendees, culminating in the question of whether, indeed, God's door will open if one knocks on it. "What if He's out of town?" Bailey asks. "What if He goes out to lunch?" After further debate on whether or not God can quit his post the scene closes this way.

> "He'll answer. He'll do it this instant if we honestly seek."
> Montjoy was agitated.
> "A sincere knock you mean," Bailey said.
> "Yes, I mean that."
> Pale, his face raised, Montjoy lifted a hand, and the knuckles tapped noiselessly against air. Carwyle and Pickney stood to knock. Casto stood and knocked but kept a hand on his throat. Hinton stood and knocked.
> When Boots came in, they were still knocking. (128)

An instance of the comic facet of Montjoy's search occurs when he's giving Guy an account of his being called, which occurred in a Washington, D.C., cafeteria and is a parody of the Pauline conversion on the road to Damascus. "'I remember what I was eating,'" Montjoy said. "'I had a dish of brown betty. . . . My spoon had actually punctured the crust, and at that instant I heard in the very beat of my blood the voice of the ineffable. Ever since I've had a reverential feeling for brown betty'" (199).

At another more terrifying extreme in the overtly spiritual concerns of the book lies the image of the soul a politician dreams recurrently. He is confined to the mysterious "third floor," where especially disruptive patients are sent; he confides his dream to Montjoy, who recounts it tersely. "'. . . His soul is stretched between two electrical poles. God's wrath crackles the length of it, bursting it into blue flames. The soul twists and screams between the relentless poles'" (154). Montjoy dismisses the vision ("'Nonsense,' I told him. 'God is love.'") more easily than we are likely to, and certainly more easily than Mayben, who immediately shifts from the wrath of the celestial Father to the sadism of his own terrestrial one. "'Even as he whipped me,'" Mayben says, "'I loved him because I knew he was just and punishing me correctly. I used to thank him for whipping me'" (155).

At the other end of the spectrum is Guy's meeting with Lotte, their fondling being the closest he comes to sexual consummation in the novel. In its tender openness, pleasant personal engagement, and potential abandon it contrasts sharply with the manipulative and coarse attempt Guy makes ("a terrible, sickening yearning," the narrator calls it) to force Lucy into his bed during her first visit, in chapter 24. This contrast highlights the failure of Guy's marriage, both in the immediate context, and over its long, unsatisfying history. Guy and Lotte have hardly begun their lovemaking, however, before it's brought up short, at least for Guy.

> He ... pushed down her pajama pants and his own. As she stepped from each leg, she held to his shoulders. He put his arms around her and kissed her mouth.
> Their teeth touched. He felt a shifting. She pulled away and in shadows made an adjustment.
> "What is it?" he asked.
> "Don't be quite so aggressive."
> "What'd you do to your mouth?"
> "My teeth."
> "What's the matter with your teeth?"
> "There's nothing the matter. There can't be because I don't have them any longer." (244)

Lotte's response is laughter, and her subsequent comments indicate an acceptance of her aging body and her self. The implication is that she would have no trouble resuming the fun. But Guy is a long way from her stage of accommodation; opposed to the experiences Lotte has been telling him about from her past, he has a lot of unlived life yet to confront and work through. The narrator's four words are like bells tolling for Guy: "His hands dropped away." From this point, he is unable any longer to ignore his condition.

Guy Dion enters Westview armed with bromides indicative of the paucity of his conscious life. In the novel's opening paragraphs he thinks, "I must put my house in order," and "I will draw on my great resources." On the drive to the hospital the routine continues: "The thing to do was enter the situation with good spirits" (11), and "The secret of life was learning not to force the harvest" (11). When his shoulders sag in a moment of inattention in his room after lunch the first day, he straightens and tells himself, "No gloomy thoughts" (38). Such statements are related to his buried psychic patterns much as a cartoon condensation of a complex novel (*War and Peace,* say) is to its original.

In any event, they do him no good. Almost immediately he is caught up in a pattern of irritation and denial, his anger and attempts at self-control woven with his continuing assertions, both to himself and nearly everyone else, that he's not sick. He not only denies his illness, he also denies his mortality: "[H]e'd not considered dying as a part of a normal man's life, something to be lived with like ripening grain or the darkness after sun. Rather death to him was a black and sinister country he would trod only the edge of and never step into" (138–39).

As I have suggested, part of the source of Guy Dion's difficulties is his attempt to live only in his persona. Not only are there numerous instances of Dion's rage, but also of his propensity to suppress his emotions in accord with the image of himself he has fought to make his true identity, the external facade into which he has channeled his psychic energy. He measures his identity wholly in terms of what he thinks is expected of an executive, of images of manliness and authority. This, too, pervades the novel until Guy's assignation with Lotte Richter.

Hoffman accumulates Guy's persona through allusion as the novel progresses. It is a familiar one. He has given away his primary attention to an image of himself as a high-powered executive whose success as founder and leader of his communications firm has brought him recognition in *Fortune*. "'I could have made it in Philadelphia or New York,'" he tells the magazine's interviewer, "'but I wanted to be where bones of my people lie in the ground'" (4). It is into the shell of the executive in his office that he frequently wishes to return as his hospital experience lengthens and the parts of his psychic life that he has neglected assert their dismantling energy within him. This aspect of his persona reasserts itself during his colleague Bart Brevet's visit. "God," Guy thinks, "there was nothing among men like the bonds of business and money" (206). He has also made part of his persona the image of the perfect father, running his family much as he runs the business, bringing to bear on it as well another aspect of his facade, the terms and habits of the Air Corps officer. Among his daughter's nicknames for him are Chief (3, 187), Governor (4, 186), and Captain (5). Socially he is a member of the country club and the Cavalier Club, has played golf and hunted foxes, and has been sought after by women.

Perhaps the portrait of himself that Hoffman has him note as he descends the stairs at the opening of the novel focuses this composite image as well as any passage:

> . . . [I]n the duskiness his portrait seemed to shimmer, his face square and strong, his black hair wavy, his powerful hands cupped over the bone handle of his whip.

> Women had fallen in love with him because of that picture. A
> bold young widow had pushed hot fingers inside his shirt and
> tugged at hairs of his chest as if ringing for a servant. (3)

Moreover, he pressures both his children to live their personae
rather than face their inner needs honestly. He forces Dibs, whose
marriage is a shambles, to promise to "make it up" with her husband
at any cost. "'[T]he family is everything,'" he tells her when she visits
him (190), in the context of everyone's grievous problems a rendingly
ironic statement. He imposes his ideal image of the family and how
children should live up to it on his son as well. In chapter 36, in his
letter requesting help he outlines his sense of how DeWitt's life
should progress. "'As you know,'" he writes, "'I want you to finish
your degree [at Yale], serve your time in the military, and come into
the business. Especially for Old Virginia Communications I'd like you
to have all the credentials because before I retire I'd be pleased and
happy to see you sitting in my chair and at my desk'" (197).

He continues in the rest of the letter to imagine the phases of his
son's life as repetitions of his own. When Guy and DeWitt come together briefly after Guy's escape from Westview, Hoffman presents
the younger man as somewhat more independent than his father's
projected version of him has prepared us for; there are indications
that he may not suffer the same kind of psychological distress his father has brought on himself. Indicative of his general perceptiveness
is his question aimed at Guy's persona-ridden experience: "'Okay,
you're forcing me to say it, but do you really do everything for Dibs
and me or are we part of the accouterments—like the house, the
Cadillac, and the memberships at your clubs?'" (286).

Hoffman clearly suggests, nonetheless, that both Dibs and DeWitt
are wounded by their father's inordinate stress on accommodation of
one's psyche to the demands of social, business, and family success,
at the expense of his internal needs.

It is at the ribald and unsettling meeting of his real teeth with
Lotte's false ones that Guy's defenses against the truths he has been
fleeing crumble. Though this appears sudden, it is the point at which
all the pressure of the novel's accumulated evidence breaks through
the dam Guy has built against it. Lotte's teeth are the culmination of a
pattern that includes the constant presence of the other patients'
variously destroyed lives (especially those of Guy's two old friends,
Cooley and Moon), the corruption of the hospital staff and the inef-

fectual pretenses of its doctors, the untrustworthy behavior of his wife, the betrayal of his colleagues, the potential breakup of his daughter's marriage. The novel moves toward this instant as inexorably as the flight of a bullet.

But it takes the particular emphasis of this intimate meeting to shake Guy loose. He encounters false teeth, a *part* of something that should be whole. The context is sexual, primary in itself as well as central to Guy's sense of his role in the world. Moreover, Lotte is the last of his mental images from the past that has not been tested by the reality of flesh and bone in the present—in the terms of the novel's title, the last of his dreams to die. The sappy language when they first speak in the gazebo evokes the doomed romantic shimmer Guy has carried with him for at least thirty years.

> "If you knew how many times I've thought of you."
> "I do know. Lotte knows."
> "I dreamed a million dreams."
> "I never stopped dreaming. I saved them like flowers pressed in a book." (236)

The kiss, then, does a lot more—or is more precise in its effects—than simply show Guy that he and Lotte are getting old, the way people do. For Guy, it is the end of the illusion of wholeness on which he has based his externally oriented life. It is a literal experience of how things fall apart: Lotte's teeth move; they can be adjusted (and adjusted to). The language of "a million dreams" undergoes a radical change.

> "Like jalopies," he said.
> "What?"
> "Like jalopies we lose bits and pieces of ourselves along the way."
> "I'm no jalopy."
> "Like old Fords and Chevys we drop the parts." (245)

Again, Lotte's response is jocular, part of the way Hoffman draws her amiable acceptance of the extrusions of her mortality. For Dion, though, there's nothing funny about it. He's stunned, undone. He has a moment of anguished memory of Lotte's "quickness and youth" that makes him want to "cup his hands over her to keep and protect her" (246), but the Annex alarms are sounding and he has to leave.

Subsequently Guy Dion sees much of the world in images of brokenness, pieces, shattered parts. The central instance of this is his vision of Lotte's body blowing apart, the image of the extractable teeth extended to its logical extreme.

> Guy stood under an oak. He looked along the length of the mall and into the sky where clouds drew into wisps. Lotte inside the bubble floated into his mind—she wearing a short yellow dress, posing, a heel lifted, one knee bent inward. She smiled and pressed the membrane. Then in the blue of the sky the bubble burst. She came apart, causing pieces to fall through space—an arm, a breast, her stocking covering a skeleton bone, her grin blooming from a toothless mouth. (249)

In the next chapter (43), counterpointed with Montjoy's account of the loss of his pulpit, the pieces of Lotte's body revolve in Guy's mind and intrude on his external perceptions as well. "In the flowered design of the carpet Guy saw tangles of Lotte's dark hair. . . . [He] looked from the rug to the window. In the black panes he saw Lotte's eyeless sockets" (252).

Hoffman has some of Montjoy's comments play on the same theme. "'God may be fashioning you to His ends,'" he says, and slightly later, more to the point, "'Man has to be broken to the final truth that all life is betrayal and loss'" (251). This reduction is Montjoy's, and however directly the image of brokenness echoes Guy's immediate perceptions, Hoffman, finally, does not strand him in such an arid conclusion. His focus for Guy is different. Even after Guy repulses Montjoy's sexual advances and kicks him in the face, he uses his handkerchief to clean the blood from Montjoy's nose. "He felt sorry for everybody who came apart, which was everybody" (256).

Not only has Hoffman used most of the behavioral content of the novel to weaken Guy's illusions, he has aimed some of its imagery at his revelation of parts and brokenness the kiss occasions. As a prelude to this focus, he gives early hints of the nature of the experience Guy has entered upon. At his first meal he notices that the "group was, to speak charitably, queer and disturbing" (33). Later the same day, after he has placed his hand on Annie Ailey's knee, he thinks that "[i]n a place like Westview irrationality was in the air. One could feel the shifting of values as if ground were giving way" (42). As he has trouble sleeping that night he has the "sensation [the bed] was slowly turning. He was certain the sensation was caused by his disjointed day, enough to upset anyone" (61). After the prelude, which is "disturbing" (literally *to upset, demolish*), "shifting," "disjointed," and "upset," Hoffman focuses this pattern more exactly on brokenness. After his second sexual move toward a nurse, Guy is sure it has been brought on partly by "the breaking of routine" (63). Cooley revels in taking the starch out of the nurses in his seductions: "'You know, watch them come apart'" (85). Barney Moon uses the same phrase when he refers to Guy's condition as their little orgy begins: "'All I heard was that you were coming apart'" (163). When the patient called Falkoner dives into the swimming pool he executes all the moves perfectly until "at the last instant everything came to pieces" (144). Montjoy accompanies his serving of the Rainbow bread at Communion with the rubric "'This is my body which has been broken for you'" (126), and he reaches the conclusion (repeated later in Guy's room) that "'a man has to be broken for God'" (204). Although Guy exempts himself from the image at the time, he sees at Westview "the men moving across shards of broken dreams" (101).

Finally, Hoffman pervades the novel with people seen partially, an arm or a shoulder or a torso appearing synecdochically so often that one ceases to notice that he is controlling perception in this way. It becomes habitual. In two places this is especially effective. First, Cooper's body as he talks to Guy from the mist in the tennis chapter (14) is seen piecemeal. Guy "stared into the mist. He couldn't see Cooper. A hand materialized" (73). Then "an arm seemingly detached moved through mist in a slow circle," and an instant later, "Cooper's head went past, no body beneath it" (74). Secondly, Hoffman has Guy see Lotte in such a way when they meet at the gazebo *before* the kiss, suggesting at first the romantic aura of the tryst, but undoing that almost simultaneously in the context of brokenness and Guy's image of jalopies that directly follows. A couple of representative images would include his first perceptions of her: "[H]e stared into darkness. A small white hand passed through a slat of light" (235); and "he saw a cheek and the tip of her nose" (236). Hoffman manages the scene this way in the partial darkness, until Guy is "ready" to see Lotte, placing his hands on her neck and moving her "until her entire face was in sunlight" (243). The kiss ensues.

All these instances precede the image of Lotte blown apart; Hoffman spaces them carefully so they are evident but not obtrusive. Thematically, they range widely from the theological to the sexual to the psychological, as well as evoking the quotidian aspect of hospital life. The most startling occurrence *after* the image of the bubble bursting, however, *is* obtrusive, both because of its complex centrality to the pattern it is part of, and its significance to the narrative's development.

During an evening showing of *Mary Poppins,* Cooley causes a diversion so that Guy may escape from Westview. Hoffman places the following passage just before Guy departs through a French window:

> "Who pulled the plug?" Boots asked. "Give me the plug."
> In the blackness humped forms moved about, but Jerry still stood close to Guy.
> "Turn on the lights!"
> "Who's got the plug?" Boots shouted.
> There were whistles, stomping of slippered feet, and chairs turning over. For an instant the projector switched on. Black shapes swept through Mary Poppins. Her Technicolor mouth closed on a dusky forehead. Again the projector cut off. (267–68)

The image of Mary Poppins's mouth acts as a magnet for much of the thematic and imagistic material that precedes it: the atmosphere of sexual innuendo and tension (and overt suggestion of fellatio [144]) at Westview, the repeated scenes involving meals and mastication in the dining room, and the overall emphasis on human appetite the mouth is explicitly associated with. It is also a grotesque parody of Guy's kissing Lotte, grotesque enough per se, and an instance of chaos similar to Lotte's exploding bubble, involving a confusion of bodies and furniture, and the scrambling of darkness and light.

Just prior to the chaos of Guy's escape, when he has been sent to the third floor because of Cletus's misinterpretation of the episode with Montjoy, a brief but telling exchange takes place between Cletus and Guy Dion. Guy says, "'[W]hatever I am, I belong to me,'" to which the doctor responds, condescendingly, "'That's a very primitive attitude'" (260). His evaluation is correct, but his tone shows he has no idea how to handle his insight therapeutically; by this time in the novel no one expects Cletus to be helpful to anybody. Dion's assertion is the primitive declaration of the primacy of the subject, the "I Am" of being. It signals that Guy has begun to discard the domination of his persona; it indicates the courage it takes to seek one's true self. Hoffman's wording here also suggests that beyond the assertion of being and subjectivity Guy has no idea who he is. This is an *enactment* of Dr. Sisler's earlier statement, "A man has to know he's sick before he can be cured" (182), even though it is made in the context of

Guy Dion's continuing denial of his illness. His way of knowing is not cerebral, but existential; Hoffman's choice here indicates a final—and, given the drift of the novel, predictable—repudiation of the inept parody of analytical procedures of the hospital. It is a fake, harmful psychology the doctors practice, a persona itself. No less than his own persona, Guy must cast it off.

Three instances, then, focus Guy's condition at the time of his escape: his loss of his illusion that things, including himself, are whole and invulnerable to dismemberment, centered in his images of Lotte's teeth and her exploded bubble; the revelation of a chaotic and perverted environment in the midst of which healing becomes impossible, centered in the image of Mary Poppins's mouth; the assertion of his primitive existence as a being more fundamental and complex than his own persona and the terms of the hospital physicians can account for, centered in his exchange with Dr. Cletus.

When he leaves the hospital he thus takes his first step toward a cure, which is to say toward psychic harmony. He is ready to risk a confrontation with himself, to see the face he has never shown the world because he has covered it with the persona. This means that Guy has to acknowledge his responsibility, which he does, admitting his illness ("'I realize now I was sicker than I thought'" [303]), and moving into despair, apology, and grief during his brief meetings with Bart Brevet and his family after he escapes from Westview. Eventually he leaves both his business and his family behind, literally a fugitive now not from himself but from society's institutions, setting out for the coal-mining area of western Virginia where he was born. He begins the lifelong engagement of learning to live with his unconscious needs, his weaknesses, and his hidden impulses.

Guy shifts from the promptings of the external requirements of his persona to a growing personal intuition, his newly discovered guide. It leads him to seek his father. As he drives through Richmond he is uncertain for a while where he is going. He considers alternatives, almost choosing to hide in the wooded recesses of a park, but "at the last instant he sped on because he realized there was only one place he could run. He'd known it all along" (308).

Although this knowing does not reach Guy Dion's consciousness until he has taken the necessary steps toward it, it has been present in his perception, and therefore in the fiber of the narrative, from the book's earliest pages. As Lucy drives him to Westview he notices "[a]head, over a pasture and trees, . . . the indistinct outline of a mountain." He squints "to focus on its shape," finding it "not rounded, not femalishly formed, but a peak with a bluish cast" (12).

Guy imagines this mountain, the first of two images whose recurrences Hoffman uses to imply both Guy's needs and his progress toward confronting them. It does not exist outside of his perception of it. The focus on the masculine aspect of its form associates its presence eventually with Guy's father, though at its initial appearance here one is not aware of how central the mountain will become. It recurs periodically, being "visible" from the window in Guy's room. From that vantage he contemplates its changing color at different times of the day. On his fifth day at the hospital, Dr. Cletus attempts to enlighten him about his mountain.

> "Ask yourself a question," Cletus said. "Why do you see a mountain?"
> "I don't know what you mean."
> "The mountain you mentioned. From your room or any room it can't be seen. I regret to say it's not there." (148)

Guy hurries back to his room from this session and, to his stark surprise, finds the mountain gone. This marks the inception of Guy's doubts about his familiar version of himself: "If he were wrong about the mountain, how many more things weren't as he believed?" (150). Later he sees it again, beginning a phase of its alternating presence and absence over the next few weeks. After his meeting with Lotte and his vision of her dismemberment the mountain briefly resumes its centrality in his perception, suggesting he has been forced back to the source of his problem and of its potential solution. "If only he could rouse himself. He should be taking action, but it was so easy to sink in his chair and look over oaks to the mountain" (250).

Following Guy's exile to the third floor the projected mountain does not recur; it is finally replaced by the physical mountain in western Virginia toward which Guy drives his Cadillac.

That Hoffman is aiming Guy's possible recovery—and the novel— at this mountain is strongly suggested on the first night Guy spends at Westview. He likens falling asleep to the time "he fell off the side of the mountain and his father caught him" (107). The most detailed memory Hoffman gives Guy in the novel follows this association. He recalls having returned only once "to the mountain" after his mother divorced his father. "He rode a train over the savage land of western Virginia, his skin becoming grimy from the coal smoke" (107). He spends an unspecified time in the coal town his father had built, living with him in "the white cottage which was full of gaps left by the mother. His father did the cooking. Guy followed him during the day to the company office, the sheds, and the tipple where cleaning machinery spiraled up black dust" (107).

On a Friday afternoon, Guy accompanies his father into the mine, deep into the mountain.

> As Guy went deeper into the mine, he thought of the mountain above him, all that terrible darkness of rock and earth which could bury him forever, and he was frightened. Trembling gave way to quaking. He was unable to keep his body still. His feet turned him and ran him—bolted him along the black haulway, over the sulphuric puddles, past the spectre faces to the golden sunlight of the entry and the world. (107)

In the evening his father seeks to reassure him. "'There's nothing shameful about fright,'" he says. "'It's the running.'" Guy responds by saying he wants to go home. "'This is your home,'" his father replies. Guy ends the exchange with "'I'm no grubby hillbilly'" (108) and leaves, as he thinks, for good.

This primary repudiation of both his father and his origins returns to haunt him, however, beginning before he is committed to the hospital. "During the last months he'd been over that scene many times. For years he'd gone without thinking of his father at all. Now it was as if the father were still calling him back into the blackness of the mountain and he himself were trying to find the entry and the sun" (108). At the spot where Hoffman places this memory, Guy's effort is still displaced. Instead of continuing to imagine an escape from the mine, he needs to conceive of himself as moving toward it. This cannot occur, however, until the brittle veneer of his persona, which includes Guy's "dream" of Lotte, has been shattered.

The second pattern of imagery in A Death of Dreams, involving darkness, shadows, and the general implication of an insubstantiality of forms, also receives a focus in Guy's memory of the mine. There it centers on his fear of being buried by "all that terrible darkness of rock and earth"; along with the mountain, it can be considered chronologically in Guy's life as the ground of his flight from himself.

The shifting of his psychic energy into a persona diametrically opposed to the image of a "hillbilly" begins here. But before Guy actually returns to Boone, Hoffman embodies that lurking darkness thoroughly in the perceptual world of the novel.

It is a more pervasive and subtle presence than the mountain, and the sketch that follows does little justice to Hoffman's skill in presenting it. He starts immediately, having Guy's portrait seem "to shimmer" in "the duskiness" of the parlor (3). Guy sees the neighbor's Great Dane, who has knocked over the stone figure of Dionysus, "prowling shadows" (6). On the way to Westview he notes a fieldstone wall "laid through the depths of oak shadows" (12), a coasting hawk throws its shadow on the grass (13), and the mansion itself is first perceived at "the end of the tube of blooming shade" (14). The first nurse Guy sees emerges "from shadows" (15).

The richness of suggestion in these few instances, introductory to the larger pattern they take part in, is remarkable. Even as we see a chief example of Guy's persona in the portrait, it is qualified by the dark force that is associated with its regressive inception, to the center of which Guy must return. Similarly, the animal that has broken the statue of Dionysus prowls the penumbra, suggesting again the primary force that will break Guy Dion, but which will be curative as well as destructive. And the "tube" through which the Cadillac moves toward the mansion suggests, as the context clarifies in Guy's memory of the mine, his flight to "the sun" and thus gives us an idea quite early that Westview is not the place where he will regain his psychic harmony. Finally, the predation and menace the hawk casts over Guy's arrival at the hospital give a sharp clue to the nature of the place, as well as to what Guy needs to face in himself.

The pattern expands to include the patients who try to escape through the oak woods surrounding Westview, into which Guy penetrates on his first nature walk (see especially p. 98). His old friend Cooley appears first as "another shape, like a shadow moving in oil" (78), and seems "to carry a duskiness with him" (79). Barney Moon, before the orgy, stands outside Guy's window "on the darkest grass. . . . [He] was a part of the night" (151).

Chapter 14, which I have discussed in another context, involving Guy's tennis "game" with Cooper, extends the shadow imagery to include mist and its scumbling of shapes, taking its place beside the shadowy disjunction of Lotte's body in the gazebo, and bringing into a sort of palimpsest the patterns of shadow, darkness, and dismemberment. Lucy is included in this procedure, too: "Reaching her was like trying to capture mist in one's palm" (132).

If one considers shadow not as light obscured but as darkness thinned, then the pattern of shadow imagery constitutes an environment of constant invitation to Guy Dion. It suggests a transition between the false clarity of the persona he fights desperately to perpetuate, and the absolute darkness he must enter before he can know and accept himself as a creature helpless before chaos. The shadowy, misty world inhabited by everyone else in the novel is Guy's way into that darkness. It is simultaneously beckoning and seductive, fearful and repulsive. Hoffman presents this complexity, and Guy's ambivalent response to it, with extraordinary fidelity.[3]

The pattern of shadow images reaches its climax in the confusion at the showing of *Mary Poppins,* during which Guy escapes. The actual disruption of the occasion, and the archetypal context the image of Mary Poppins's mouth embeds it in, make further development of the pattern impossible. What remains, then, is the darkness Guy has been fleeing since his trip with his father into the mine. Guy accepts the constant, surrounding invitation to enter it as he stands in the yard outside his house in Richmond.

> Guy stepped in front of the window. Lucy sighted him first. She spoke his name and stood. Dibs also stood and removed the cigarette from her mouth. The girls closed to her for protection. DeWitt tossed back his hair. They were all in the light on the other side of the glass while Guy stood in darkness and saw they were afraid to have him home. (302)

He then takes the Cadillac and drives through "a tube of darkness" to Boone.

The novel's final chapter is masterly in its economy, both in Hoffman's rendering of the local detail of the dead town, and his calling up of the hospital experience preceding it. The environment of the

---

3. The imagery of shadow and mist is a pattern, but it is not schematic. Hoffman has embedded these perceptions in context and character, making it a seamless part of his fabric. Such procedure is common to his work in general, and renders the term *realism* not even an approximately accurate label for his fiction. He is "realistic" as René Magritte and Edward Hopper were, his books employing the visual precision and sharpness of dreams, shifting at odd times, becoming oblique at unexpected junctures, leading toward an implicit richness of underlife that the work, say, of Sinclair Lewis or John Galsworthy seems to me to lack.

ghost town contrasts in all its stark, Spartan particulars with Westview, and Guy becomes one with the old place. He is the poor, bare, forked animal itself. Lost, his car abandoned, he gives himself up to the wilderness as if it were a guide. "He crossed a hump in the road and allowed the tilt of the land to carry him forward"; he follows a stream and later, at its junction with a railroad, decides "[a]ll he had to do was follow the tracks" (313). He wonders not what someone will think of him in his current condition, but rather "[w]hat would he say to his father?" (311). In the midst of Boone, ramshackle, deserted, he meets an old man, a former miner who has stayed on to die with the town. "'I was beginning to think I was alone in the world,'" Guy says (316).

> Still the old man did not speak.
> "Do you work here?" Guy asked.
> "Nobody works here," the old man answered.
> He stacked the board on his wheelbarrow. His fingers were curved to handles he no longer held.
> "Then everybody—"
> "I'm everybody. The mine's closed." (316)

Guy does not actually enter the mine again, but Hoffman writes a series of passages to indicate a parallel experience. The old man leads Guy into the "cavernous" remains of the commissary where he lives. They cross two thresholds into an inner room. "'Wait,'" the old man says.

> His match blew out, and he walked into darkness. He returned holding a lighted lantern, his elongated shape sliding across walls. With the lantern he led Guy to the rear of the commissary and into a vacant storeroom sprinkled with rat droppings. . . .
>
> The old man carried the lantern into the third room, this one small, fitted with an iron stove, a cot, and a green table on which was a white porcelain washbowl and a pitcher. An oval mirror hung from a nail. The window was dark. (319)

This progress echoes the journey inside the mountain from Guy's boyhood visit with his father.

During the night this procedure of confrontation with his sources and his self continues. He prays, though "none of the Presbyterian prayers he'd been taught as a boy" (323). Instead, "[t]he only words he could think of were, God, please care for all people in wind and cold" (323). His dozing is punctuated by the old man's fitful breathing and the rapping of the stove as it cools. Later the wind wakes him and, despairing of everything, he cries "like a child, . . . his fingers over and in his mouth to choke the noise" (324). The old man is not his guide or his doctor or his father, but he functions temporarily as their surrogate, tending Guy's basic physical needs as a companion, without intrusion on the self.

I do not mean to imply *A Death of Dreams* shifts into the mode of fairy tale. It does not, though there are clearly archetypal elements at work in the meeting with the old man. Guy comes to the first open opportunity for psychic restoration. He is not changed, however, but given back access to himself. His will and determination remain, but they are redirected. Hoffman has him think again, as he did at the novel's outset, "I must put my house in order" (322). Now the phrase has what it lacked initially—context and direction centered not in the superficies of persona but in the awful complexity of the self struggling to engage its darkest recesses. It is clearly related to his father: "After we're reconciled, I'll think of ways to put my house in order" (324). His priorities have been reordered. It's a beginning, small but crucial, and hard-won. There is no guarantee, of course, that Guy will persevere, but the odds, and the narrative disposition, seem to favor that prognosis. His refusal to accept the old man's prophetic, Everyman stance—"'Surely the people is grass'" (323)—and his declining to "quit" and slowly decay with the town, indicate his predilection.

I would add, finally, a third stage to the role of the narrative voice in the novel. At first Hoffman uses it to set up the familiar conflict between an individual and an institution. This modulates quickly into its second function, the more complicated struggle within Guy Dion, becoming more tightly associated with his psychic restoration. As the patterns that point through brokenness toward that restoration gradually reach Guy's best opportunity, the voice shifts again, abandoning its early stages of external derangement and interior chaos. In its attempt to fulfill an increasingly accessible aim it becomes less self-conscious and less self-seeking in Guy's behalf. The voice compelling the narrative enters the service, so to speak, of a vision—and, implicitly, a time—beyond the narrative. As the possibility of truth emerges from under layers of deception, the voice becomes, finally, like fate, subservient to the outcome whose potential it creates. Guy is freed to search, perhaps futilely, for his father. The book is free to end.

The death of dreams here, then, is healthy. It is a death of illusions, "dreams" in the sense of worldly ambitions tailored according to formulae that preexist the specific self, "dreams" of future glory or fulfillment through behavior adjusted to ideal configurations, reductive scenarios the human psyche forever invents to deceive itself with, instances of its inveterate vulnerability to its own evasions.

Dreams in the other meaning, the unconsciouss's delivering up to awareness of its unavoidable needs—the best instances of which are Guy's mountain and his vision of the dismembered Lotte—are what is born of Guy Dion's experience in the enabling circumstances of this novel. It could as well have been titled *The Birth of a Self.*

Faith and Time

William Hoffman's View of the Future in *The Dark Mountains*

Martha E. Cook

In his fourth novel, *The Dark Mountains* (1963), William Hoffman emphasizes the setting both of place, the coal-mining region of Hoffman's native West Virginia, and of time, the period of the Depression. As Ernest E. Leisy notes in his comprehensive 1950 study *The American Historical Novel,* "in America—so rapid are changes here—a generation appears sufficient to render a preceding period historical."[1] In the twentieth century change has been so rapid that each succeeding *decade* has rendered the previous one historical. Thus Hoffman's setting determines the particular genre of a given novel.

Yet, rather than fulfill the historical novel reader's expectations by depicting chronologically the rise of a poor boy to prosperity and power through hard work and determination, Hoffman revises the traditional plot of the American dream and reorders time to illustrate the necessity of adapting to the changing mores of the modern world. For Hoffman in *The Dark Mountains* the rugged individualism of Scottish immigrant James MacGlauglin deteriorates into lawlessness; his grandson-in-law Paul Crittenden becomes the hero for a new era through his ability to work within the confines of society and government. Both James and Paul, as well as Paul's wife, Faith, illustrate the seminal definition by Georg Lukács of "the specifically historical" as "derivation of the individuality of characters from the historical peculiarity of their age."[2]

Hoffman's purpose in challenging the reader's expectations through his plot, to project a future significantly different from the past, is evident in the climactic scene near the conclusion. James MacGlauglin has dominated the masculine world of his mountain community with his firm individualism, his deep belief in God, his love for his family, his desire for control, and his willingness to use violence to oppose change. Yet he has failed in his attempt to defy the federal government and the National Labor Relations Board and keep the unions out of his

1. Ernest E. Leisy, *The American Historical Novel* (Norman: University of Oklahoma Press, 1950), 5.
2. Georg Lukács, *The Historical Novel,* trans. Hannah Mitchell and Stanley Mitchell (Boston: Beacon Press, 1963), 19.

mines. The conflict has escalated to the point where he must rein in his paramilitary force and surrender to the National Guard or risk the total destruction of his beloved mansion and possible loss of family members. James waits on his terrace, straight and proud, the MacGlauglin family united with him: Sarah St. George, his only surviving child, stands by her father's side; her son, Jamie, stands on his grandfather's other side, with his wife, Flora, behind and apart from him; Sarah's daughter, Faith, stands beside her husband, Paul Crittenden, with his arm around her. James falls with a stroke as he walks toward the soldiers and dies a few days later. Through his farewells to the members of his family, one sees his vision of the future with his grandson, Jamie, in the position he has held. However, Hoffman, by manipulating the order of events in the novel, has actually given the characters of Faith and Paul, a woman and an outsider, the values, abilities, and opportunities to succeed in the world of the future, where individuals must exist within society rather than as antagonists to it.

The novel opens at a point a few years before the time of this final episode. The events of that time period begin with the introduction of Richmonder Paul Crittenden to the alien world of the mountains and unfold through his making himself essential to James's coal-mining business and establishing a home and family with Faith. Paul will be in the foreground of the events of the novel and the future projected from the nonviolent resolution of the conflict between James and the union. However, Hoffman uses him at first to draw the reader into the isolated mountain community, where "the terrain had an unsettled, violent appearance," the buildings in the coal camp "appear grimy, cheap, and temporary" (5), and the mansion "sat like a fortress on the crest of a hill" (6).

While it is clear that Paul and the MacGlauglin grandson, Jamie, have an important past, Hoffman delays giving the details for a time, focusing in the second chapter on the young woman Faith. Her complexity is obvious. She is nurturing as she works in the animal infirmary she has set up in the old stable, yet she is overly sensitive to the animals' suffering and prone to extreme emotional states: "Sometimes she would imagine a cloud was gathering over her—an evil black cloud which wanted to hurt her" (9). The source of her instability is not yet defined, though one learns that she has seen evidence of violence by Jamie and actually witnessed her grandfather's beating a miner. In these early chapters the emphasis is on Faith's alcoholic father, William St. George, instead of her mother. Faith is drawn to his weakness rather than to her mother's strength, seeing him as sensitive and intelligent, her as hard and uncaring.

Sarah is, in fact, introduced through the perspective of her now-estranged husband, William. Except for a brief glance, the reader sees her first just as William did, "chopping wood": "A stout, healthy girl, she handled the ax as expertly as any man. . . . Good peasant stock, he thought. Good breeding stock" (19). His own mother was not a strong woman, so it seems he is drawn to Sarah's strength. While she appears "stiff, undemonstrative" (23), she responds to William sexually. Eventually he moves her to Richmond, but he thinks she ruins their life there because she does not support and defend him; he also blames others for his failure to perform as expected at the Yellow Dog Mine. However, Hoffman withholds the details of these episodes.

Before Hoffman describes Paul's struggle to acclimate himself to the work of the mine, he tells James's story, against which any physical struggle or demonstration of ambition by another character will pale. The Scottish immigrant boy, skilled as a mason, learns engineering in New York City shortly after the Civil War, moves up to a position as vice president of a railroad, and at forty starts over, eventually building a tunnel through a mountain in West Virginia so that his own coal can be hauled to market. James sends to Scotland for a wife who will bear the sons he desires. His family selects Sarah MacDonald, whose credentials are those traits of character he values: "she was industrious and clean and lived in fear of the Lord" (46). He sees her as "a woman to help him endure" (47). When James tells Sarah he wants to take her from her comfortable home in Louisville to a cabin in West Virginia to start a new life, she replies, "'I've come across an ocean. I suppose I can go into mountains.'" Then he finds "at long last his real love for her" (55). She survives a brutal winter, only to die of a fever the next spring. James subsequently loses his first son, Angus, in a conflict over a miner's wife and his second, his namesake, in a mine fire. The episode of Angus's conflict with the miner Scanlon, father of the union organizer, sets in motion the events of the present time in the novel. At this point in the text it seems that James and his struggle to maintain dominion over the world he has created constitute Hoffman's central concern.

Hoffman then develops Jamie MacGlauglin St. George's character through an account of his personal history, beginning with his relationship with Paul. Jamie's college days, filled with hunting, drinking, and womanizing, culminate in his importing a West Virginia prostitute for the graduation party he gives for Paul. While Faith mistakes her father's weakness for sensitivity, Jamie fights to prove there is no St. George weakness in him. Earlier Sarah has resorted to abuse to try to save Jamie from the fate of her older brother. After a Faulknerian scene in which sixteen-year-old Jamie is lost in the woods and forced to eat raw meat to live, he is finally able to confront his mother, throwing a bear's head at her and proclaiming, "'I'm free of you'" (122). Through the deaths of the MacGlauglin sons, the weak character of William, and the violence and excessive appetites of Jamie, Hoffman leaves space in his plot for the emerging roles of Sarah, Faith, and Paul in the future of the MacGlauglin family.

As *The Dark Mountains* continues, Paul Crittenden's character quickly grows in significance. Like William St. George, he possesses the formal education and culture that the MacGlauglin men lack. But he also has physical strength, commitment, and ambition, as illustrated by his ability to learn the physical work in the mine at which William failed. At this point Hoffman, in an indication of Faith's importance to Paul, reveals more details of Faith's past, primarily the story of her first marriage to Darryl Carter. Sent to a traditional boarding school in Virginia, Faith falls in love with a boy from town. Brought back to the mountains, she perseveres, keeping in touch with him and eventually arranging to elope from the Presbyterian women's college in South Carolina where her mother has thought she will be safe. However, the long arm of MacGlauglin money and influence locates the couple in a hotel in St. Louis. After Hoffman shows how one of James's men beats up the husband, he shifts to a scene from the present in the plot of the novel and then to a series of episodes from the distant past, to help the reader understand the characters of James and Sarah and shed light on this harsh treatment of Faith.

Thus Hoffman uses James's conducting Presbyterian church services in MacGlauglin as a vivid example of his desire for control over every aspect of the lives of his family and the miners. Next he depicts Sarah's courtship and marriage and the birth of Jamie. Absent the aid of a doctor or even a midwife, Sarah cuts the cord herself and clears the baby's mouth so he can cry, producing a powerful image of her courage and strength. Her father proclaims, "'You're a MacGlauglin, all right'" (176). Here Hoffman fills in the details of Sarah and William's experiences in Richmond to emphasize her strength in contrast to his weakness. William buys an old house in the country; Sarah works hard, as she always has, to make a home for their family and tries to fit into the society he loves; he remains impractical and extravagant. When she finally realizes he is having an affair, she can at last "see him the way he was" (182). Without telling him she is again pregnant, she returns to her father's mansion, where the sickly Faith is born. Sarah gives her daughter this symbolic name because she believes her prayers that her child live have been answered.

When describing how William returns and is allowed to live at the mansion, too, Hoffman elaborates on a crucial incident that has been alluded to twice, in a reference to James's loss of his second son and in a description of William's defensive attitude toward the Mac-Glauglins. The truth is that he is a coward who ran from the Yellow Dog Mine fire in which young James MacGlauglin died. Though Sarah tells William he must leave James's home, he refuses and subsequently, in the ultimate display of weakness, rapes her because she has refused to share his bed. The ironic meaning of his name St. George, with its connotations of bravery, is apparent: William is no hero in this tale. These insights focus the reader's attention on the contrasting strength of Sarah's character. However, Sarah's return to the mansion ensures that she will remain in the shadow of her father and that Jamie and Faith will be raised in a world he rules. Sarah suffers over the trials of her children: "Her cross was to have handled her children wrongly. Just as she had attempted to protect Jamie, she had also hoped to keep Faith from throwing her life away" (190). Still, her extreme responses to her children and her desire for control weaken her role.

Finally Hoffman returns to the episode of Faith's marriage. The revelation that she suffered a breakdown after the beating of her husband and had to be hospitalized for a year explains her emotional precariousness and her inevitable siding with her father. Unaware of his true character, she has been made all too aware of the negative power exerted by her mother and grandfather. Faith is seriously wounded by this ordeal. A few months after her return to the mansion, "she started going down into the camp in order to visit the sick. She seemed to search out suffering." Then she begins "to collect animals" (191). At this point in her life the reader actually meets Faith for the first time; given this background of her emotional condition, one comes to understand her character and see possibilities for growth.

Paul's influence with James MacGlauglin is strengthened as he moves from physical labor in the mines to the accounting area, where he is able with wit and intelligence to move James toward modernity.

He institutes new, efficient methods and purchases up-to-date equipment. James remains skeptical until Paul saves him in an audit by the Bureau of Internal Revenue. Paul in turn learns the technical aspects of mining from reading books and questioning Jamie, who like his grandfather loves the life of the mountains and the mines. Jamie's traits are those valued in the traditional masculine world of the MacGlauglins, and Paul's are not, yet Paul gradually gains the respect of James MacGlauglin.

Probably because Paul is so different from her grandfather and brother, he also gains the love of Faith. Faith has been trapped in the fortress of the mansion since returning from the hospital; Jamie, whose own view is quite narrow, opens up her horizons by bringing Paul into her world. She first really notices him when he blisters his hands in the mines, instinctively responding to his suffering. Her feelings come into focus when he encounters her in the garden while she is transfixed by the image of a grasshopper being stung to death by a wasp. Paul comforts her; she reacts in a way he does not expect, by kissing him. He realizes, "There was nothing restrained or maidenly about the way she did it" (205). Faith is the one who first says to Paul, "'I'm quite certain I'm in love with you'" (208). He is not aware at this point, as the reader is, of her earlier experiences with Darryl.

Paul does not believe he is in love with Faith and fears hurting her. He leaves for a visit to Richmond, where he realizes he no longer has feelings for his old girlfriend, and returns to the mountains with mixed emotions, wanting to resume his work, but also to tell Faith that he does not want to marry her. Before he can speak, Sarah calls him in. She tells him she knows Faith's feelings for him, explains Faith's history with Darryl and her breakdown, and urges him to "'think clearly,'" mentioning the MacGlauglin wealth. When Paul accuses her of trying to buy him, she replies, "'There are worse things. . . . I'd rather buy you than have my daughter hurt irreparably. If you're worried about romance, forget it. It means nothing. Even I had romance'" (217). While Sarah is attempting to continue to exercise control over the family as James has done, her actual power over her children has diminished as they have grown older. Paul tells Faith he does not want to marry her, so she offers to be his mistress: "'I don't know what sort of mistress I'd be, but I'm willing to try. Don't take everything from me, Paul.'" As he comforts her, he becomes "filled with a great tenderness," for "[i]f what he felt wasn't love, it was indeed very close to it" (218).

A scene of the bawdy events leading up to Faith and Paul's wedding ceremony reinforces the need for the kind of stability and common sense that Paul can bring to the MacGlauglin family, even though he briefly falls under Jamie's influence. The strength of Faith's love and her determination to make her marriage succeed are firmly established when on their honeymoon she whispers to herself about Paul: "'I love you. . . . I'm going to make you love me'" (244). Knowing that Paul does not love Faith as she loves him, the reader is gratified by the positive experiences of the honeymoon in Miami, where Faith demonstrates her desire to make a home for Paul. On their return, she is determined to move him—and her father—to the old St. George house where they can establish their own family away from the MacGlauglin mansion. As they work to refurbish it, their relationship grows stronger. Hoffman uses a warmly humorous scene to show how comfortable the two have become together. They spontaneously make love on an old spool bed; when it collapses beneath them, "they held each other and laughed until they became weak" (252). Faith turns from her animals to her own growing family, and her pregnancy creates a closer tie between her and Paul.

Having laid the foundation for a solid future for Paul and Faith, Hoffman returns briefly to what seems to be the central conflict of *The Dark Mountains,* that of James and the union. Then he focuses again on the MacGlauglin family, showing Sarah sending someone to spy on Faith—who reports only that "'Mrs. Faith's happy as I ever seen her'" (262)—and then turning her attention to Jamie, trying to manipulate him into settling down. She arranges for Jamie to visit the daughter of James's friend and rival Moses Bailey; he returns early with an unexplained black eye, saying only, "'You might as well give up on me'" (266). Having again proclaimed himself free of Sarah, Jamie is determined to make his own choices. So Sarah turns back to Faith. In desperation over her daughter's coldness, Sarah goes uninvited to her home, greeting her, "'I'd like to come in and see my grandson'" (267). She then pleads, "'You've always been kind to everyone. Be kind to me as well'" (268). As Faith begins to exhibit emotion, the baby cries out. Sarah is able to save him from choking, mirroring her action at the birth of her own son. She quietly withdraws, but Faith runs to her to express her gratitude. Sarah realizes, "It wouldn't be easy for them. It would require a long time. Yet they had made a start. She felt as if she had been shrived" (270). Hoffman allows Sarah to let go of her desire for control yet still exhibit her characteristic courage.

Next Hoffman returns to Jamie to reveal the circumstances of his black eye. Thus the story of his relationship with Flora unfolds. Flora is Moses Bailey's secretary, who has a room in his home; Jamie wrongly assumes that she is Moses' mistress as well. He sees her as "a real woman," but she is paradoxical: painted fingernails and voluptuousness juxtaposed with an old-fashioned hairdo and "old-maid schoolteacher" shoes (277). Jamie thinks, "First of all, she was a big piece. He'd always preferred big females. Secondly, she had that hint of a slattern about her. High-class ladies were generally complicated. They wanted to talk more than do it" (280–81). However, Flora proves complicated. She dresses and dances seductively, yet makes clear to Jamie that "'marrying's what it's going to take'" (283) before she will have a sexual relationship with him. Unexpectedly, Flora's behavior is a clear contrast to Faith's less traditional behavior with Paul.

The reader has already seen how Jamie, since age thirteen, has openly enjoyed sex with a variety of women and even brought a Sintown prostitute named Lilly to the party he threw to celebrate Paul's graduation. Apparently he has never before met a woman who did not respond to his desires—or whom he could not buy. When Jamie proposes to Flora, she calls his bluff by insisting on meeting his family. To Jamie's astonishment, Flora arrives dressed in "a dark suit which was both fashionable and demure," wearing "no make-up." At dinner, dressed in a white gown, "She seemed almost stately" (287). When Flora continues to hold out for the wedding, Jamie in frustration seeks out Lilly, now a successful madam, but still "tall and slim as a boy," still hidden behind "a mask of make-up" (292). After a wild, expensive weekend with her, he returns to settle down in wedlock with Flora.

In chapter 22 Hoffman straightforwardly accelerates the plot. The opening sentence reads, "James MacGlauglin had a sense of things going wrong" (293). Though James has seemed to be at the center of events, the weight of attention to family affairs over which he has little control has diminished both his personal power and the force of the masculine world he represents. The pressure to cooperate with the union grows as labor candidates are successful in the state elections. Hoffman portrays James in such a way as to make the conflict with the union a complex one. James truly believes he acts justly, and there is no evidence that he cuts corners to make money and thus endangers the miners unduly. The issue that energizes the miners at MacGlauglin is one of individual choice: he has not even allowed them to choose what color they paint their houses.

Symbolically, other things go wrong. James's health gradually declines. Paul pressures him to modernize the operation of the mines, for example, "to replace mules with motors" (296). As mules give way to tractors when the agrarian way of life passes, so the loss of the mules at the mines represents a dramatic step towards modernism. The close relationship between a man and his work dissolves with the introduction of the machine, just as the power of the individual mine owner is giving way to the group—the union and the state and federal governments that lie behind it. Paul comes to realize that "[t]he old man was a lot more stubborn than any of his mules" (304). In Lukács's terms, both James's intransigence and Paul's flexibility are derived from the conflict between tradition and change characteristic of their historical period, a conflict that has emerged as far greater than the local conflict of James with the union.

From this point to the conclusion of *The Dark Mountains* in chapter 28, Hoffman follows strict chronological order. Having established the basic characters and accelerated the conflict, he no longer needs to reorder time; his plot moves inexorably toward the future. Violence and vandalism continue, with Jamie at the forefront. At the same time Paul sees Jamie changing in his private life: Flora "had Jamie obeying her like a trained poodle. Occasionally he looked as if he couldn't understand what had happened to him." From Paul's perspective, "[i]f ever a male deserved such retaliation, Jamie did" (310). James agrees to a meeting with Scanlon, the union organizer, but is recalcitrant. Jamie wants to use physical force, but Paul and James restrain him. James uncharacteristically—weakly—blames Paul for his being outmaneuvered. As Paul observes how events are affecting James economically, he realizes "the only way out was to come to terms with the union. Since the union offered a standard contract, James MacGlauglin would be neither better nor worse off than hundreds of other owners signing up. One gallant, stubborn old man could not hold out against the overpowering social change which was sweeping the whole country" (314–15). Typically, Paul is pragmatic about change while still acknowledging the virtues represented by James's attitude.

Hoffman continues to focus on the conflict with the union and the consequent violence. Before long James is called before the National

Labor Relations Board. Paul, trying to intervene for James, recognizes the lesser stature of the district director of the NLRB. He "could not imagine the nasty little bureaucrat ever going into a wilderness to develop an entire community and industry. He might have lasted a day" (326). Paul is no doubt correct; yet he is sensible, working with the company lawyer to understand that James's defiance can result in imprisonment, as he then explains to Jamie. James attends the hearing but behaves like a dictator. Though he comes to believe that he has enough loyal miners to defeat a vote for the union, historical forces are on the side of the union.

Following the election, James retreats into solitude; Jamie, into drink. It is "left to Paul to hold things together" (334), a phrase that clearly foreshadows the future. In a startling move, James determines to sell the mines and, in the meantime, to close them, provoking a court order, as Paul has tried to explain such an action will. James imports firearms, evicts the remaining miners, and organizes an armed force of mountain men. Evoking another time of rapid change, Hoffman writes: "Paul believed some of the old men whose fathers had followed Jackson or Longstreet must have confused the word 'union' with Yankee government instead of labor" (343). Thus Hoffman reminds his reader that James's resistance to change is part of a larger resistance of the South to enter the modern world. A battle ensues, and the union supporters are temporarily vanquished. As the mansion becomes "a hospital," there is a role in the plot for Faith, who "moved among the hurt. She gave them water and wiped their brows" (348–49). As she earlier left behind her animals for the job of building a family, she now moves outside her family to play a significant role in the community. While Faith's role seems traditional from the perspective of the 1990s, she has grown in independence far beyond her grandmothers and her mother. Like Paul's character—and James's—hers derives, in Lukács's terms, from the historical time in which she lives.

The scene in which James testifies before a Senate committee in Washington is very realistic. He stands firm, and the senators hold their own narrow, provincial views. For a time, "Public opinion was overwhelmingly against him, yet a few papers began to voice a grudging admiration for what one termed 'a man who has the courage to stand up for his convictions'" (358). However, James goes too far, styling himself as one chosen by God "'to lead the rest'" (360). He leaves the hearing with the admonition that he will be held in contempt for doing so. Back in the mountains, violence continues, and

James's world narrows to the mansion, which literally becomes the fortress predicted in the opening scene, though Faith continues to help the wounded there. Finally the governor calls out the National Guard. The general in charge treats James with respect, making his ultimate decision easier.

At this point, the climactic scene I described earlier occurs. James would have surrendered to the federal government, represented by the National Guard, had his body not given out. As James lies ill, Sarah nurses him and Paul works on his behalf to sell the mines. Their positions are clear: Sarah "had always been his right arm," and "[h]e knew the young man would do the best he could" (372–73). After his second stroke, James calls in each family member in turn. Faith is first, with young Paul. James expresses his strong regard for family: "'I must tell you it has caused me happiness that you and your mother have become reconciled. . . . You are a good woman and have my blessing'" (374). Then he asks to kiss the child. Next is Paul, who has persevered and obtained an offer for the mines. "'You are like a son,'" James says. When he asks Paul to convert to his own Presbyterianism, Paul agrees. To Flora, he says, "'Have babies.'" And he reminds Jamie that he will one day be "'the head of this family.'" Acknowledging the role Sarah has played in his life, James speaks warmly: "'You are my first love. I ask you to be strong in the faith that we will again be together. . . . Know that I have loved you better than my life'" (373–75). At the end, both sides of James's character are evident. To his assembled family, he says, "'I have loved you all,'" but at the sight of the mountains, he proclaims dominion and ownership: "'Mine! . . . Mine . . .'" (376).

Though the word *mine* with its dual meanings closes the novel, James's attitudes die with him. Sarah, so much like her father, has a new role as grandmother, but not a place in public life or the life of the community. Jamie may nominally head the family, but his and Flora's roles are clearly limited by their provincialism. Jamie lacks the ambition and discipline to carry on his grandfather's work and the imagination to chart a new course. Paul is the one equipped to move ahead in the modern world, and he has Faith beside him to balance his strength and vision with sensitivity and caring. Freed by the sale of the mines, they can make their own life in the new wilderness of machines and government.

William Hoffman has brilliantly plotted the novel *The Dark Mountains,* and the historical setting of particular events of the Depression in the mountains of West Virginia provides rich material for his development of themes of individuality and community. A strictly chronological depiction of the events in the novel would have focused the reader's attention squarely on the inevitability of the downfall of James MacGlauglin and his way of life, given his character and the facts of history. However, Hoffman uses unexpected shifts in time and perspective to move subtly but powerfully the sphere of influence from James, who sees only what one individual with strength and ambition can accomplish, to Paul and Faith, who stand together as a family and are willing to work within the community and the larger society to promote change.

Throughout *The Dark Mountains* Hoffman raises questions to which he delays answers until the reader is prepared to understand the possibilities of the future. Issues of unionization transcend particular historical events to become part of the movement towards modernism in the first half of the twentieth century. Likewise, life in the mountains can transcend the darkness of James MacGlauglin's masculine world. In a discussion of James Fenimore Cooper's character Pathfinder, James E. Swearingen and Joanne Cutting-Gray speak of "the power of fiction to refigure the world."[3] While history reaches its inevitable conclusion, Hoffman's narrative strategy in *The Dark Mountains* produces a fiction that only seems to close with the death of one man in his time, but actually opens up the possibilities for a family in new times that lie ahead. Through revising the traditional plot of the American novel, William Hoffman has indeed reconfigured the mountain world he loves, for his original readers of the 1960s and for those in succeeding decades.

3. James E. Swearingen and Joanne Cutting-Gray, "Cooper's Pathfinder: Revising Historical Understanding," *New Literary History* 23 (spring 1992): 267.

A Modern Parable

Sowing and Reaping in *Furors Die*

Jeanne R. Nostrandt

William Hoffman returns to the locale of West Virginia, the place of his birth, for his tenth novel, *Furors Die* (1990). It is the story of two boys who grow up on opposite sides of town and whose lives, personalities, and characters are polar opposites: Wylie DuVal, from the "right" side, and Amos "Pinky" Cody, from the "wrong" side. Even their names reveal something about their place in the story: *DuVal,* with its connotation of an old, civilized heritage, combines with *Wylie* and its intimation of sly or cunning; *Cody,* with its connotation of Buffalo Bill and the early American spirit, combines with *Amos* and its reminiscence of the Old Testament Hebrew prophet. His peers, however, know Amos as "Pinky," suggestive of an effete and diluted quality, neither pure white nor blood red. This dual connotation of names parallels the dual nature of the character and the two sides of himself Pinky has difficulty reconciling.

In a larger sense, this is the story of two sides of the American character—the cultivated gentleman and the rough-edged pioneer; it is the story of the motivations, wits, and drives within the human character, drives often unknown even to the person whose actions they instigate. Underlying the story line is the implied question of both the source and the necessity for a moral standard. The literary theme is at least as old as narrative itself and, in American literature, is characteristic of such disparate fiction as that of James Fenimore Cooper with his Leatherstocking tales and William Faulkner in his classic *Absalom, Absalom!* Hoffman, however, sets his microscopic eye on a 1990s examination of the theme as both an American anomaly and as an aspect of the human condition. His investigation weaves a parable for readers of contemporary times.

The novel has three parts, which divide the story much as they would a three-act play. Hoffman's stint as playwright-in-residence at the Barter Theatre in Abingdon, Virginia, influences both style and structure in his writing, especially in this novel. Book 1, as in a drama's prologue, introduces the central figures and reveals their emerging characters. Wylie and Pinky meet during their sixteenth year, finish at the exclusive White Oak School for boys together (a situation manipulated by Wylie's father, for whom Pinky worked), and face their future lives as apparent enemies after Pinky becomes the butt of a practical joke played by Wylie and his school chums. Book 2, the rising action, begins during the summer before the boys attend college; Pinky finds work to supplement the college scholarship he received, and Wylie sows his wild oats in travels with three friends in Europe. The second book ends at the pinnacle of the rising action; the young men have matured into their lives and seem to be worldly successful beyond their imaginings. At the opening of book 3, the men and their peers have taken their places as pillars of their community, and the stage is set for the falling action with its denouement and resolution. The drama ends, but the tragic implications of the parable exhort the reader to examine his own time and place.

Unlike the ancient Greek tragedies in which the hero falls from his high position through some personal flaw, recognizing his own complicity in his downfall, this 1990s narrative has no clear hero. Hoffman depicts a time and place in which the values and standards that would define a hero are out of rhythm. It is a familiar theme in Hoffman's writing: he develops a character who seems to embody all the virtues on which the American society claims to structure itself, only (later) to show that character as unsuccessful in his pursuit of the American dream because either the society fails him, his own flaws prove too strong, or both. The proverbial "American Dream" is itself on trial in this novel, as it is in much of Hoffman's work. The faults, then, according to Hoffman, are in the characters as well as their construct, the society. Hoffman implicitly asks: "Does the society really promote and value the one who starts at the bottom, rises by his own energies and wits, and becomes materially successful? If it does, should it? And where does morality find its roots in that society?" Hoffman seems to say that the passions—the furors—that forged a country out of wilderness, as did the early pioneers, will reach a termination or burnout point. If the inheritors lack the same burning energy of their forebears, or if they lack the vision and the values of those forebears, they appear doomed to failure, according to Hoffman. Then furors die.

The small unnamed town in West Virginia's Kanawha River valley is a town of workers (mostly miners) and owners, the haves and the have-nots. When the story opens, the town is experiencing its last gasps; coal mining has ceased to be the black god it was in the thirties and forties. Hoffman himself grew up in a similar environment, his own great grandfather connected to the mining industry. Hoffman's realistic and haunting descriptions of place grow out of memories from those early years. Using poetic descriptions almost unparalleled in contemporary fiction, Hoffman creates the town and the industry in realistic detail:

> Tugs bullied coal barges around red and black buoys. The tugs' whistles sounded like ocean liners. After a rain the river would clean itself to wanness, but then coal washings upstream again wove dark curls into the flow.
>
> On the other side of the valley the C&O passenger trains slid fast along the hill-shadowed tracks. Slovenly coal drags clanked monotonously, their whistles steaming. Often the valley trembled with the trumpeting of locomotives and tugs.
>
> Toward the west the factory chimneys shot hot black discharges into the summer sky and filled the valley with a twilight haze. People in the city hardly noticed the smoke unless they left and came back, the return like entering an infernal region. Wylie's father had an explanation.
>
> "Where there's no smoke, there's no human endeavor." (14–15)

This is the point at which Hoffman's story begins. Readers can imagine a nineteenth-century generation of immigrants who came to America with a dream to succeed, followed the dream and built the foundations and industries that solidified America's economy; they can imagine a first or second generation of descendants who survive an economic depression in the 1930s and rebuild their businesses on more solid footing, often by grasping the opportunities arising out of the demands of war and economic fluctuation. Those same industries that were the brainchildren of the immigrants' and their descendants' dreams operate on the labor of the followers as well as the labor of the leaders, the dreamers. Wylie's father, then, could say, "'Where there's no smoke, there's no human endeavor.'"

The young people, Wylie and his crowd, have no inkling of the history behind their comfortable lifestyle, much less of anything dying. In their innocence they live fast and play hard at the Pinnacle Rock Club where their parents are lifelong members. The world that their grandfathers carved out of the mountains and that their fathers refined in the valley seems permanently secure and long-lasting to them. They plan to live happily ever after. Then enters Pinky Cody, the catalyst who stirs up things so that they never again will be the same.

Amos "Pinky" Cody is the outsider brought into the Pinnacle Rock Club's young circle by one of the girls who was bored by the monotony of her comfort and security. Hoffman introduces him on the first page of the story—the redheaded, pink-skinned, smirk-faced boy from the wrong side, rubbing shoulders with the blonds and brunettes, their peaches-and-cream complexions tanned to perfection. His pink appearance, though, sparks excitement into the group as a lighted match would in a pile of dry driftwood. His obvious superiority is in his diving; he performs to perfection the one dive Wylie's crowd practices to master, the half gainer. In his climb to the high board, Pinky effects the nonchalant, effortless, but competent attitude that characterizes him all his life. In his perfect, self-styled execution of the dive, he impresses his audience, from the club members celebrating the Fourth of July down to the white-jacketed waiters: "Time slowed till the dive was transformed into a ballet of spiraling body so lingering that he appeared to break laws of gravity and motion" (3). Perhaps Hoffman chooses the time, the celebration of America's birth with its parties and fireworks, to remind the reader of the risks of too much comfort and complacency in a society built on the ideals of hard work and earned rewards—the Puritan ethic. Hoffman's introduction of Pinky, however, into this self-satisfied world is not only prophetic, but also ironic, and Pinky's entrance incites the normally dormant furors of the club's young members to action.

Wylie's father and his generation, who have lived in luxurious mansions along the riverfront, homes constructed by their fathers as they built the mines and mills, reluctantly abandon those houses. They build newer luxury in homes high on the surrounding mountains, across the river and above the line of billowing smoke and clouds of smog in the valley. "'I guess the rich can't stand to breathe the same air [as] the rest of us,'" Pinky says to Wylie (15). As they move to higher ground, many of the poorer inhabitants, mill laborers and miners who work in the very mountains above whose heads the mine owners build, move into the renovated, abandoned homes as renters. Ironically, most of those laborers who came down out of the hills to work the mines and mills cannot afford to leave the valley's smog and live on those same hills. Hoffman does not ignore the images of the haunted, coal-smeared faces. When their furors rise, they appear throughout the novel as climbers over the walls of the country club during celebrations, as clients of the lawyer Pinky, as disabled workers grouped together in Broken Men, Inc., and as union leaders fighting for a stronger voice in contracts and negotiations.

Hoffman's perception transforms life into a series of concentric circles in his narrative. Coal is the instigating force in the history of the town, but it lies dormant deep in the mountains until the visions and energies (furors) of men bring it into daylight and create a demand for it. As long as it is in demand, life around it hums: visionaries build the factories and mines to hire the laborers; laborers come down from the mountains to work the mines and mills; both groups build homes near the site of their work until they pollute the environment; to escape pollution, the builders move onto the mountains from which the laborers had come, and the laborers move into the abandoned houses in the town. Hoffman's first circle, rooted in the coal-rich mountains, comes full circle.

The next round, its root still firmly planted deep in the earth's coal mines, concerns the inheritance (concrete and abstract) of the generation coming of age in the West Virginia town, Wylie and his crowd. The older generation, Wylie's father and his peers, inherited not only the homes and industries from their fathers, but a sense of responsibility and duty, a kind of noblesse oblige. Hoffman gives many instances of this trait in the story; one is when Mr. DuVal witnesses a policeman in the street attempting to arrest a staggering drunk from whom others have recoiled, rescues the unknown man, and gets a taxi to take him home—an act of "kindness and charity," says Pinky. That readers later learn the man was Pinky's father (and that Pinky's father is a World War II hero) is an example of life's synchronisms and surprises Hoffman is apt to employ in his fiction. Another instance of Mr. DuVal's sense of duty to the less fortunate is his hiring of Pinky as handyman after Pinky came to his office and offered his services. Though no work was available, Pinky makes his own jobs and performs his work even before he is salaried. This kind of ambition Mr. DuVal respects, and he hopes the trait will influence his own son. He hires Pinky and then puts Wylie to work beside him during that summer.

This same man feels an obligation to attend his church each Sunday because he is a role model for his community, but he feels no obligation to perform other responsibilities the church deems desirable. In a letter Wylie finds after his father's death, Mr. DuVal articulates his beliefs: "I've not been a religious person, but I've always believed in decency and fairness to my fellow man. It seems to me those two values are as good as any to build a life upon" (206). Wylie learns from this as well as from his upbringing the importance of a civilized human obligation, if not a religious value: "More than anything else his father had championed the goodness in men, the quality which Wylie intended to make the center of his own life" (206).

Hoffman depicts DuVal's charity as rooted in his character rather than in any doctrine. He questions, however, how that sense of noble obligation, charity, or values gets passed on to the next generation.

In addition to his legal inheritance, Wylie finds bundles of money and mementos along with the letter in his father's office. DuVal's principles become clear in the letter: "The money in the box I've kept around for emergencies. . . . It should be reported as part of my estate. You don't want any battles with the revenue people, who always win" (206). He reminds Wylie of his duty to care for his mother and of a five-thousand-dollar legacy to Miss Burdette, his secretary. Later Wylie makes her the executive vice president of the Elk Land and Lumber Co.—built by his grandfather, passed to his father and on to him—because she best knows how to run the business. When Wylie later is surprised by knowledge from an offhand remark by his mother that Miss Burdette was his father's mistress for years, Hoffman demonstrates an essential operating principle characteristic of that generation—civilized and polite people did not discuss such things in public or in their homes, except in the most private of circumstances. Also significant to Hoffman's technique is the fact that adults throughout the novel usually appear as their surnames or titles—Mr. DuVal, Miss Burdette, my father, or Pinky's mother—and only the next generation, Wylie and his crowd, act under their given names. Such considerations seem anachronistic to a 1990s reader inured by television talk shows in which guests discuss the salacious details of their lives before the entire world, and when most people in a 1990s society address one another by given names. Hoffman's style is reminiscent of a time when a better taste prevailed, courtesy had meaning, and, though some secrets went to the grave, lives were richer for the difference. At the same time, he reminds the reader of the complexity of the human condition through a revelation of this man's virtues as well as his vices, the duality in all men's natures. In fact, most of his characters reveal multiple facets of themselves, and their complexity derives from the competing factions within each. Hoffman does not pass judgment on any. The second circle completes itself with the deaths and retirements of DuVal's generation. His final words in his letter best reveal that generation's hopes for the sons and daughters who will inherit what it has built: "When I leave this world, I will live on in you. Think well of me. I have loved you dearly" (206).

Wylie and his group understand their futures in this same community, taking over the control where their fathers leave it. While they foresee no place for the Pinkys of the town in their leadership positions, Hoffman sees this intrusion as a necessary ingredient for the town's survival. The wealthy young people go away to a school that will give them the necessary education and polish to return as productive members of their community, but they lack any understanding of the work and sacrifice of building and maintaining that town. They learn the proper manner of actions, dress, and speech from their parents, their schools, and their churches, but they do not learn about their own characters and the values by which they must live. Hoffman suggests that each of these institutions—parents, schools, churches—neglects the power inherent in them to teach values along with lessons for material success.

Amos "Pinky" Cody, however, is always around to remind the townspeople and readers of the necessity of values. At first he is Amos, the prophet, like Elijah, crying in the wilderness, "Prepare Ye the way of the Lord." His constant, adolescent, holier-than-thou attitude and his exhortations for his peers to repent, though, turn away all with whom he comes in contact. Wylie is the only exception, and he stays close only because his father has made it his duty to do so. Amos's concept of religious fervor (furor) stems from his wild, half-crazed mother, who speaks in the eclectic Pentecostal language of her offbeat church and who dedicated her son to that church at birth. Amos believes for much of his life that this way is his destiny. When he strays from the way, Hoffman brings in the mad mother to remind him of his dedication, much as the ancient Greeks might use the chorus or the androgynous soothsayer Tiresias in their dramas to warn tragic heroes of wrong choices. Placed at strategic times in his story, her haggard figure appears as his conscience when he goes out with his first girl, goes away to school, rides off to college, and joins the Episcopal Church. Hoffman suggests that these times in life are times of choices, times when Amos might stray from the right path or might lose his direction. While he also implies that these experiences can teach or reinforce the values Amos needs for his life, Hoffman does not show him as victim. Amos has the personal responsibility to make his own choices and to suffer the consequences.

Hoffman's third circle surrounds the generation including Wylie and Pinky; still rooted in the mines, its circumference extends farther

than others before it. The danger of clever and knowledgeable ma-
nipulations without wisdom and ethics as driving forces is at its center. At the opening of book 3, Pinky's mother appears in Wylie's
stockbroker office: "'My temple is not a house of trade!'" she screams
(221). Her image is apocalyptic; she is a modern-day Elijah, as
Hoffman brings her onstage for a final warning:

> Her fingers were lifted above her head as if lightning would
> zigzag from the tips. She was disordered, her dark hair tangled,
> her skin splotched, her purple dress torn at the hem. She wore
> not stockings but rolled-down white socks and sandals. Her legs
> needed shaving. On her head was set a warped hat which had
> once been decorated with artificial flowers. Only stubble re-
> mained. Her white gloves were ripped at the fingers and soiled.
> Her wild smoky eyes seemed lidless.
>   "Repent!" she shouted. "Bend your knee to the Lord!" (221)

Wylie, with the smiling demeanor of his class and profession, greets
her cordially: "'Hello, Mrs. Cody, how good to see you'" (222).

The comedy apparent in the juxtaposing of Wylie's mannered but
insincere approach with the crazed but prophetic mutterings is another characteristic of Hoffman's work. His usually subtle but often
hilarious humor sprinkles his fiction and relieves the weight of the
dark scenes. When he presents the poor-boy image of Pinky in his
hot, dark woolen suit on a summer day, his red hair wild, his ignorance obvious in such actions as his drinking the finger-bowl liquid
when invited to the DuVals' home for dinner, Hoffman intentionally
elicits laughter. When he has Pinky stroll with a kind of swagger and a
smirk on his ruddy face into the crowd at the club on his first visit,
Hoffman means for the reader to smile at the funny, thinly disguised
facade Pinky affects. These comic images, however, also demonstrate
the starting point in the distance Pinky must travel to become the
character as he last appears. Not only does the comedy make the serious more palatable, but it makes the import of Hoffman's message
and the character's evolution more evident. The reader may not want
to laugh at the disheveled woman and her ravings but will surely see
her as a lunatic. Hoffman introduces comedy, expecting the laughter
to relax the reader's tension and open the receptivity to a more essential revelation, the seed of truth in the woman's ravings.

When Pinky comes to Wylie's office to collect her, she tells him:
"'You are besotted with sin!'" (223). Hoffman's keen ear for the lyrical

quality of language is apparent; he uses his knowledge of the hill people's tongue, with its echoes of Middle English, alongside the refined speech of the DuVals. When he wants to demonstrate the ordinary speech of churchmen, he might differentiate among denominations by expressions and tone more than pronunciations. Anne's father, a former middle-class Protestant minister, asks Wylie, "'Are you a Christian man?'" and "'Will you repeat the Apostles' Creed with me?'" (165–66); Father Bonney, the Episcopal priest, says to Wylie: "'Surely you consider yourself a Christian and don't believe we can live without a conviction of immortality, which is the true basis of morality'" (241). When Pinky first meets Wylie outside his father's office, Pinky tackles him and speaks in his earnest ecclesiastic voice: "'Repent and give you [*sic*] life up to Him.' . . . 'Think of the thief on the cross'" (6). Hoffman's ear for subtlety in tone, style, and language as means of differentiating social status is characteristic of his fiction. His use of "furors" in the novel's title implies anger, a force that destroys, but it is also synonymous with energies and fires, forces necessary for creating.

The optimal creation in Hoffman's novel, however, is Amos "Pinky" Cody. Prototypes of this kind of character might be Thomas Sutpen in William Faulkner's *Absalom, Absalom!* or Willie Stark in Robert Penn Warren's *All the King's Men,* or even Willy Loman in Arthur Miller's *Death of a Salesman.* At the same time, Pinky has unique qualities that make him an original. The first image of the insolent, lanky figure coming out of his shantytown life into the Pinnacle Rock Club celebration to demonstrate the half gainer, his one accomplishment, is not unlike the initial image of Faulkner's Sutpen, the barefoot boy directed to the rear door, away from the front door of the wealthy man's house by the black servant. Humorous though the images may be, both boys' fear and shame instigate a determination (furors) to improve their lot. Pinky, however, seems to rise out of the environment in which he lives—the tall and stately mountains, the once fertile but now polluted valley, and the dark, coal-dusty mines. His furors burn atop his red head as equally as the fires spew from the mine's coal stacks. Similarly, the poor and ignorant but intelligent and ambitious Willie Stark begins his law studies with the altruistic motive of helping his fellow man, especially those who were poor and ignorant like himself. Pinky, too, starts out with such motives, at least in his conscious efforts, and he begins his practice back in his native shanty community, assisting the underdog and the maimed to attain some measure of satisfaction. Like Willie Stark, however, Pinky becomes obsessed with his own successes and, step by step, discards those characteristics not deemed befitting a successful man.

Pinky is an opportunist. The first step of his journey to the top of the mountain begins when he learns of Mr. DuVal's kindness to his drunken father. Pinky, consciously or unconsciously, sees DuVal's act as a chink in his armor and an entrée for himself into DuVal's world. Seizing the chance, Pinky begins his climb, each time placing his foot on the back of someone or some event that assisted him before. At first he believes himself appointed as messenger and dedicated to God by his mother, and each rung of his climb an opportunity to call the wicked to repent. As he moves through his life, however, he adopts the qualities he observes in his enemies, finally becoming one of them. Pinky, like Sutpen, begins a design to build a better life for himself and for his descendants. Unlike Sutpen, when he too easily accommodates his plans as opportunities arise, Pinky convinces himself that his actions are not only in keeping with prevailing values for success, but that he lifts the plight of the poor man with every step he rises. Believing he has one foot in both worlds, he allows his furors to control him; he aims to beat the controllers at their own game, especially Wylie DuVal.

While spouting the platitudes of his offbeat religion, Pinky performs the art of worldly manipulation as expertly as he once performed the half gainer. Convincing those around him, those peers who had once jeered and derided him, that he has their welfare at heart and can make them all wealthy, he stoops to fraudulent methods in his greatest effort to spring to the top. Even if Hoffman had intended Pinky as a sympathetic figure, a clever imitator who fashions his life after the actions he observes in others, he ultimately brings Pinky's corrupted character to light. Like the fallen angel Satan in Milton's *Paradise Lost,* Pinky speaks much of the truth in life and displays many acts the world considers virtuous. He seems heroic until readers recognize the darkness of his character, the blackness in his soul. Pinky's furors stem from deep-seated anger and envy, and they destroy him by burning him out from the inside.

Amos Pinky Cody is the voice preaching warning to the unrepentant, a false prophet as it turns out, but not an ignorant one. He cannot plead ignorance of the knowledge necessary to redeem his spirit. Consumed with furors—his envy and greed—he ignores his primary lessons, even when his mother/conscience inserts herself into his life. Pinky Cody is the redhead among the blonds and brunettes, both separate from and a part of their lives. Genetically, the redhead is an amalgamation of the genes in a blond and a brunette, both different from and a part of both. In folklore, the redheaded child is of suspicious origin and the redheaded adult is often supernatural. Hoffman, as have numerous writers before him, makes use of Pinky's hair color in revealing his character, expecting at least a subliminal knowledge of its connotation. Pinky's last day alive reveals his failure to reconcile the multiple sides of his personality; it demonstrates the extremes to which his schizophrenic self has deteriorated. Though he succeeds in climbing to the top—his home on the top of a mountain defies gravity (the gods)—his fall is much greater for the height. Hoffman parallels his initial image of Pinky and his perfect half gainer with his final image. The first enviable dive is at the club:

> He seemed to have no intention of diving when he climbed the chrome ladder. It was more like a stroll, his lean body loose, his hands negligent, the smirk switched on, and he didn't rise far when he sprang either, yet as he arched off the board and strained his suddenly muscled physique backwards, his arms became crucified, and sunshine illumined his rigid length. (3)

Hoffman depicts the innocent Pinky as a Christ figure, crucified and ready for assumption into heaven. When he fails to live up to that potential, Hoffman illustrates the result. Pinky had no idea he would take his last dive, nor that his audience would shrink to Wylie, alone:

> As Wylie full of horror grasped the railing and looked over, Pinky fell away. He still wore the outsized sunglasses, yet Wylie saw the fear on him, terrible fear, and something else—a stab at the old swagger, the body splendor, and for a moment while Pinky dropped he tried to take control, to transform his fall into flight, or maybe a dive, a half gainer, one of those beautiful, lingering half gainers he performed off the high board at the Pinnacle Rock Club.
> Gravity was too much, the acceleration, the irresistible pinwheeling. They flung him till he relinquished his body's grace. (304–5)

Hoffman must have envisioned the angels being thrust out of heaven when he gave Pinky his last dive, when he brings his third circle to closure. At least the Greek Furies seem to perform their vengeance on him. Like the ancient Greek dramatic heroes, Amos "Pinky" Cody recognizes his complicity in his downfall—he strayed from his god and his appointed mission. Like more modern heroes—Sutpen, Willie Stark, Willy Loman—he does not understand where his plan went wrong, how he made the wrong choices or failed his dive. The denouement is only partially realized, therefore; Pinky does not fully understand his guilt in the catastrophic outcome. Hoffman sees his crime as the unethical and fraudulent actions of his life; however, he sees his besetting sin as his abandonment of his god-given mission, his giving over to his furors, greed and envy. So great was this sin that Pinky did not want merely to surpass his tormentors, to beat them at their own game; instead, he wanted to supplant them, to actually *be* Wylie DuVal. Hoffman does not condemn Pinky in his final failure; he demonstrates that Pinky is Everyman. No matter how great the potential in each person, the possibilities are of no advantage if ethical values do not accompany the actions: "What does it profit a man to gain the world if he loses his soul?" Hoffman, however, does not preach in his fiction, neither in tone nor in language. He allows the young Amos and his crazed mother to do this for him in *Furors Die*. In this dramatic fiction the resolution is open-ended, as it is in most twentieth-century writing. The house of cards Pinky built comes tumbling down, the Humpty-Dumpty stockholders fall off their walls, and Wylie is haunted in his dreams. Furors seem to die. If Hoffman offers any hope for this community, it is through Wylie, the remaining character who learns from the experience, who does recognize his own complicity in the tragedy. On the book's last page, Wylie experiences what may or may not be a final hallucination. The shadowy figure appears in a rainstorm, her arms flailing outward, her specter ominous: "Was the figure Pinky's mother hurling curses at him across the snow?" he thinks (308). Frightened into reckless driving, he slams against a stone, serpentine wall—an image reminiscent of the serpent enticing the first people, Eve and then Adam, into knowledge. Wylie bounces off the wall, bitten by the snake, as it were, and recognizes his own guilt and responsibility in the experience. His furors die as he moves toward the redeeming love of home: "He backed his car, his tires spinning, and steered with grave care around ascending curves and through the chaotic storm toward the sheltering warmth of his home and hearth" (308).

Hoffman ends his parable with an image of Wylie as a mature and wiser man, one who hears the ravings of wild and haunting prophets in a time when rock music and television volumes would drown out their voices. Wylie can discern the seed of truth in those ravings, and

Hoffman believes his readers can do likewise. His novel has all the action of a drama, the morality of a medieval play, the intrigue of a psychological thriller, the recognition and respect of a history in which mankind's furors built a nation. When furors die, he notes, the remaining artifact or ashes speak to the quality of the human endeavor that made it. The carbon that burns as coal fires energizes and enriches the valley; if left over time in the heart of the mountain, however, it becomes diamond—the angers that burn as furors energize, though they burn out the human heart. Only the redeeming quality of love can neutralize the furors in Hoffman stories. In *Furors Die,* he reminds his readers to drive "with grave care around ascending curves and through the chaotic storm." At the same time, Hoffman expects them to remember: "Where there's no smoke, there's no human endeavor."

Bibliography

Compiled by Jeanne R. Nostrandt

Primary Sources

The Trumpet Unblown. Garden City, N.Y.: Doubleday, 1955. Reprint, Greenwich, Conn.: Fawcett, 1957.

Days in the Yellow Leaf. Garden City, N.Y.: Doubleday, 1958. Reprint, Greenwich, Conn.: Fawcett, 1959.

A Place for My Head. Garden City, N.Y.: Doubleday, 1960. Reprint, Greenwich, Conn.: Fawcett, 1962.

The Dark Mountains. Garden City, N.Y.: Doubleday, 1963. Reprint, New York: Modern Literary Editions, 1969.

Yancey's War. Garden City, N.Y.: Doubleday, 1966. Reprint, Greenwich, Conn.: Fawcett, 1967.

"The Love Touch" [unpublished, produced play]. Abingdon, Va.: The Barter Theatre, August 22–27, 1967.

A Walk to the River. Garden City, N.Y.: Doubleday, 1970. London: Robert Hale, 1972. Reprint, Greenwich, Conn.: Fawcett, 1972.

A Death of Dreams. Garden City, N.Y.: Doubleday, 1973. London: Robert Hale, 1975.

Virginia Reels. Urbana: University of Illinois Press, 1978. Includes the short stories "The Spirit in Me," "Sea Tides," "The Darkened Room," "Your Hand, Your Hand," "Amazing Grace," "A Darkness on the Mountain," "A Southern Sojourn," "A Walk by the River," and "Sea Treader."

The Land That Drank the Rain. Baton Rouge: Louisiana State University Press, 1982.

Godfires. New York: Viking, 1985. Reprint, New York: Penguin Books, 1986.

By Land, by Sea. Baton Rouge: Louisiana State University Press, 1988. Includes the short stories "Fathers and Daughters," "Landfall," "Moon Lady," "Cuttings," "Smoke," "Lover," "Faces at the Window," "Moorings," "Indian Gift," "Altarpiece," "Patriot," and "The Question of Rain."

Furors Die. Baton Rouge: Louisiana State University Press, 1990.

Follow Me Home. Baton Rouge: Louisiana State University Press, 1994. Includes the short stories "Dancer," "Tides," "Coals," "Sweet Armageddon," "Boy Up a Tree," "Abide with Me," "Night Sport," "Points," "Business Trip," "The Secret Garden," and "Expiation."

Tidewater Blood. Chapel Hill, N.C.: Algonquin, 1998. Reprint, New York: HarperPaperbacks, 1999.

Doors. Columbia: University of Missouri Press, 1999. Includes the short stories "Doors," "Prodigal," "Place," "Roll Call," "Humility," "Stones," "Blood," "Landings," "Tenant," and "Winter Wheat."

Secondary Sources

Bitz, Karen. "In Celebration of the Great South." *Breeze* [James Madison University alumni magazine], October 30, 1995, 24.

Buffington, Robert. "The Intolerable Wrestle." *Modern Age* 16 (winter 1972): 109–11.

———. "Tolerating the Short Story." *Sewanee Review* 102 (fall 1994): 682–88.

Capers, Charlotte. "The Comeuppance of a Gentleman." Review of *A Place for My Head. New York Times Book Review,* April 17, 1960, 24.

Carroll, John M. *"Yancey's War." Library Journal* 91 (March 1, 1966): 1245.

Carter, Ron. "Hoffman Energizes His Tales." Review of *Follow Me Home. Richmond Times-Dispatch,* September 11, 1994, F4.

———. "Hoffman Evokes Sense of Place." Review of *Doors. Richmond Times-Dispatch,* June 17, 1999, F4.

———. "Hoffman Turns to Suspense." Review of *Tidewater Blood. Richmond Times-Dispatch,* April 12, 1999, F4.

Clark, Steve. "[Hoffman's] Novel's Success Is Thrilling News." *Richmond Times-Dispatch,* April 30, 1998, B1.

Coleman, Dero. "Compelling Novel." Review of *A Walk to the River. Dallas Times Herald,* September 13, 1970, E7.

Cooperman, Stanley. "Recent Fiction." Review of *The Trumpet Unblown. Nation* 182 (February 11, 1956): 123.

Core, George. "Confronting Dilemmas of Flesh, Spirit." *Roanoke Times and World-News,* December 5, 1993, D4.

Corwin, Philip. "Hitting the Target More Often Than Not." Review of *A Death of Dreams. Washington Post Book World,* July 6, 1973, B4.

Daniels, Lucy. "After the Past, the Present." Review of *A Place for My Head. Saturday Review* 43 (June 18, 1960): 19–20.

Davenport, Gary. "Fiction and the Furniture of Consciousness." *Sewanee Review* 100 (spring 1992): 323–30.

———. "The Fugitive Hero in New Southern Fiction." *Sewanee Review* 91 (summer 1983): 439–45.

———. "Good People in Trouble." *National Review* 22 (October 20, 1970): 1113, 1115.

Davis, Mary H. "Introduction to the Novels of William Hoffman." Master's thesis, Longwood College, Farmville, Va., 1980.

Davis, Paxton. "*Furors Die* Author Is Making Mark." *Roanoke Times and World-News,* June 10, 1990, F4.

Evory, Ann, and Linda Metzger, eds. "Hoffman, William." In *Contemporary Authors,* new rev. ser., 9:269. Detroit: Gale Research Company, 1983.

Ewell, Nathaniel MacGregor, III. "The Novels of William Hoffman." Ph.D. diss., University of South Carolina, 1975.

"Exploring Hoffman's 'Fictional World.'" *Farmville Herald,* August 31, 1988, 9A.

Frank, William. "The Fiction of William Hoffman: An Introduction." *Hollins Critic* 28 (February 1991): 1–10.

———. "Hoffman Doesn't Dodge Life." Review of *Furors Die. Farmville Herald,* March 21, 1990, A1–3.

———. "Hoffman Opens His Door." Interview. *Farmville Herald,* June 4, 1999, 1, 10.

———. "Hoffman's Novel Tight, Taut, Compelling." Review of *Tidewater Blood. Farmville Herald,* April 1, 1998, B2.

———. "Local Author Returns for New Book." Review of *Godfires. Farmville Herald,* June 26, 1985, A7.

———. "Reviewer Finds Novel 'First Rate, Engrossing, and Soul-Searching.'" Review of *A Walk to the River. Farmville Herald,* October 2, 1970.

Friddell, Guy. "A Good One for Sam." Review of *A Death of Dreams. Norfolk Virginian Pilot,* May 27, 1973.

Galloway, Gloria. "Author First Wrote Love Letters for a Fee." *Richmond Times-Dispatch,* April 7, 1968, H14.

Gatewood, Willard B., Jr. "Talented Young Writer Bares Tyrannical Life." *Rocky Mount N.C. Telegram,* April 28, 1963, B5.

Hass, V. P. "Weak Stomachs Warned: Here Is War's Horror." Review of *The Trumpet Unblown. Chicago Sunday Tribune,* January 1, 1956, pt. 4, p. 5.

Hughes, Kathleen. "Adult Fiction." Review of *Follow Me Home. Booklist* 90 (August 1994): 2022.

Johnson, Greg. "Wonderful Geographies." *Georgia Review* 43 (summer 1989): 406–16.

Kaufman, Leonard. "Tod Young of the Bleeding Heart." Review of *Days in the Yellow Leaf. New York Times Book Review,* January 26, 1958, 5.

Kiely, Robert. "Tales and Stories." Review of *Virginia Reels. New York Times Book Review,* February 25, 1979, 26.

Kneebone, John T., ed. "Virginia Books." Review of *Follow Me Home. Virginia Librarian* 40 (October–December 1994): 21.

Magill, Frank N., ed. *"Days in the Yellow Leaf."* In *Survey of Contemporary Literature,* 1780–82. Englewood Cliffs, N.J.: Salem, 1977.

Manuel, Diane. "Short Stories." Review of *By Land, by Sea. Christian Science Monitor,* March 16, 1988, 20.

Margoshes, Judith. "New Creative Writers." *Library Journal* 80 (October 1, 1955): 2146–47.

McKelway, Bill. "Surprise Ending." Review of *Tidewater Blood. Richmond Times-Dispatch,* April 29, 1998, F1.

Merritt, Robert. "Old-Fashioned Values." Review of *Furors Die. Richmond Times-Dispatch,* May 20, 1990, G5.

———. "Spirit Prevails in Well-Crafted Tales." Review of *By Land, by Sea. Richmond Times-Dispatch,* April 3, 1988, F5.

Mitgang, Herbert. "War from the Hospital-Unit Level." Review of *The Trumpet Unblown. New York Times Book Review,* January 8, 1956, 26.

Nash, Alanna. Review of *Doors. New York Times Book Review,* June 13, 1999, 21.

Neuberger, Christine. "Southside Life Inspires Author." *Richmond Times-Dispatch,* May 15, 1988, C1.

Nostrandt, Jeanne R. "[Henry] William Hoffman." In *Contemporary Fiction Writers of the South,* ed. Joseph M. Flora and Robert Bain, 222–33. Westport, Conn.: Greenwood Press, 1993.

———. "[Henry] William Hoffman." In *Southern Writers: A Biographical Dictionary,* ed. Robert Bain, Joseph M. Flora, and L. D. Rubin Jr., 228–29. Baton Rouge: Louisiana State University Press, 1979.

———. "Hoffman, William." In *Contemporary Southern Writers,* ed. Roger Matuz, 193–95. Detroit: St. James Press, 1998.

"Notes on Current Books." Review of *By Land, by Sea. Virginia Quarterly Review* 65 (winter 1989): 19.

Review of *Follow Me Home. Kirkus Review* 62 (July 15, 1994): 937.

Review of *The Trumpet Unblown. New Yorker* 31 (December 31, 1955): 55.

Review of *The Trumpet Unblown. Time* 67 (January 9, 1956): 92.

Seward, William W., Jr. "Coal King Wages War with Unions." Review of *The Dark Mountains. Norfolk Virginian Pilot,* April 28, 1963.

Shorris, Sylvia. "Literature's Stepchild." Review of *Virginia Reels. Nation* 228 (February 10, 1979): 153–54.

Spalding, Maria Blair. "Men in Trees and Men on the Water: Hoffman's Virginia Odyssey." Master's thesis, James Madison University, Harrisonburg, Va. 1997.

Steinberg, Sybil S., ed. "Forecasts." Review of *Follow Me Home*. *Publishers Weekly* 241 (August 15, 1994): 88.

Stone, Jerome. "War's Torture Chamber." Review of *The Trumpet Unblown*. *Saturday Review* 39 (January 14, 1956): 41.

Stuart, Dabney. "Engrossing Novel Tale of Two Men." Review of *Furors Die*. *Roanoke Times and World-News*, June 10, 1990, F4.

Sullivan, Brad. "*Godfires* Is about Value Struggles in Virginia." *Richmond Times-Dispatch*, July 28, 1985, F5.

Sullivan, Walter. "About Any Kind of Meanness You Can Name." *Sewanee Review* 93 (fall 1985): 649–56.

Summer, Bob. "Hoffman Tale Is Breakout for Author, House." *Publishers Weekly* 245 (February 9, 1998): 20.

Swayne, Marge. "Hoffman's Talent Is No Mystery." *Farmville Herald*, April 10, 1998, 1–2.

Tannenbaum, Earl F. "*The Dark Mountains*, by William Hoffman." *Library Journal* 88 (March 15, 1963): 1178.

———. "*A Place for My Head*, by William Hoffman." *Library Journal* 85 (March 1, 1960): 986.

Taylor, Welford D., ed. "William Hoffman." In *Virginia Authors*. Richmond: Virginia Association of Teachers of English, 1972.

Theroux, Paul. "Saint or Preacher?" Review of *A Walk to the River*. *Washington Post Book World*, October 25, 1970, 6, 13.

Treadwell, T. O. "Being a Man." Review of *The Land That Drank the Rain*. *Times Literary Supplement*, August 13, 1982, 888.

Van Ness, Gordon. "Hoffman's *Doors* Offers Look at Human Nature." Review of *Doors*. *Farmville Herald*, June 4, 1999, 8.

Waterhouse, Carole. "In Short." Review of *Godfires*. *New York Times Book Review*, July 28, 1985, 18.

Watkins, Floyd C. *The Death of Art: Black and White in the Recent Southern Novel*. Athens: University of Georgia Press, 1970.

Wilhelm, Albert E. "Fiction." Review of *Follow Me Home*. *Library Journal* 119 (August 1994): 136.

Wolf, Michele. "In Short." Review of *By Land, by Sea*. *New York Times Book Review*, May 15, 1988, 26.

Notes on the Contributors

Ron Buchanan is Chair of the Communications Technologies and Social Sciences Division of Northern Virginia Community College–Manassas Campus. Interested in such topics as rhetorical analysis, popular culture, religion, and southern literature, he has combined these subjects in previous studies of Hoffman's war novels, definition of heroism, and narrative poetics.

Fred Chappell, a native of western North Carolina, has taught English at the University of North Carolina, Greensboro, for thirty-six years. Author of a dozen books of poetry, two of short stories, and two of criticism, he has also written eight novels. His most recent work is *Look Back All the Green Valley* (Picador USA, 1999). He is currently Poet Laureate of North Carolina.

Martha E. Cook is Professor of English at Longwood College in Virginia. She has served as coeditor of *Resources for American Literary Study,* as a Fulbright lecturer at Waikato University in New Zealand, and as President of the Society for the Study of Southern Literature. She has published on southern writers ranging from Ellen Glasgow to Nikki Giovanni.

George Core has edited the *Sewanee Review* since 1973. During his editorship twenty-three stories by William Hoffman—including two in 1999—have appeared in the *Sewanee Review,* which also published Fred Chappell's essay. Core has written on Mr. Hoffman's fiction on other occasions, most recently in reviewing *Tidewater Blood* and *Doors.* His essays and reviews have appeared in a wide variety of periodicals in the United States, and he has edited five books, chiefly on the literature of the South.

William L. Frank is Professor Emeritus and former Dean of the College of Liberal Arts and Sciences at Longwood College. He has published books and articles on Sherwood Bonner, William Hoffman, Robert Penn Warren, and Allen Wier. He is currently working on a critical biography of William Hoffman.

George Garrett, author of thirty books, editor and coeditor of nineteen others, is Henry Hoyns Professor of Creative Writing at the University of Virginia. Most recently he edited *The Yellow Shoe Poets* (Louisiana State University Press, 1999). He served in Italy, Austria, and Germany in the Field Artillery of the U.S. Army.

Jeanne R. Nostrandt is a native Virginian and Professor of English at James Madison University in Harrisonburg, Virginia. Her teaching and scholarship specialty is southern American literature. She has served as Acting Head of the Department of Foreign Languages and Literatures and as Director of the Honors Program at James Madison University. In addition to her work on William Hoffman, she has published and presented papers on many American writers, including Doris Betts, Hortense Calisher, William Faulkner, Kaye Gibbons, Gail Godwin, Josephine Humphreys, Flannery O'Connor, Reynolds Price, Lee Smith, Max Steele, William Styron, and Eudora Welty.

Dabney Stuart has published sixteen books of poetry, fiction, and criticism, most recently *The Way to Cobbs Creek: Stories* (University of Missouri Press, 1997) and *Settlers: Poems* (Louisiana State University Press, 1999). His criticism includes a study of Vladimir Nabokov's novels—*The Dimensions of Parody*—and articles on the work of Fred Chappell, Franz Kafka, Thomas Traherne, and others. He has held literary fellowships from the National Endowment for the Arts, the National Endowment for the Humanities, the Guggenheim Foundation, and the Virginia Commission for the Arts. In 1979 he received the first Governor's Award for the Arts in Virginia. Since 1965 he has taught literature and writing at Washington and Lee University in Lexington, Virginia, where he is now S. Blount Mason Professor of English.

Gordon Van Ness is Associate Professor of English at Longwood College in Virginia. He has published two books on James Dickey and essays on other writers such as William Hoffman, Robinson Jeffers, and James Gould Cozzens.

Index